SINGLE DAD'S
CHRISTMAS WISH

ALISON ROBERTS

ıı Harlequin

MEDICAL ROMANCE

Special thanks and acknowledgment are given to Alison Roberts for her contribution to the Royal York Hospital miniseries.

H Harlequin®
MEDICAL ROMANCE

ISBN-13: 978-1-335-99335-9

Single Dad's Christmas Wish

Copyright © 2025 by Harlequin Enterprises ULC

H Harlequin Enterprises ULC
22 Adelaide St. West, 41st Floor
Toronto, Ontario M5H 4E3, Canada
www.Harlequin.com

HarperCollins Publishers
Macken House, 39/40 Mayor Street Upper,
Dublin 1, D01 C9W8, Ireland
www.HarperCollins.com

Printed in U.S.A.

Royal York Hospital

As the holiday season approaches, Christmas chaos descends on the Royal York Hospital and the expert medical staff find themselves caught up in a snowstorm of drama. They'll always put their patients first, and delivering Christmas miracles is something of a specialty. But as the snow falls and tensions rise, so too does the chance for unexpected encounters under the mistletoe. And they could change everything come New Year's Eve!

You won't want to miss a moment of the excitement, so join the festive celebrations in...

Single Dad's Christmas Wish
by Alison Roberts

Winter Nights with the Midwife
by Karin Baine

Both available now! And don't miss...

Mistletoe Kiss to Heal His Heart
by Annie Claydon

Christmas with Her Rival
by Becky Wicks

Wedding Date with Dr. Petrides
by Kristine Lynn

New Year to Nine-Month Surprise
by Louisa Heaton

Coming soon!

Dear Reader,

One of the things I love about writing is when I can set a story in a place I know and love. I used to rely on my memories and photographs or souvenir books to take me back somewhere, but with today's technology, I can actually walk down the streets and go inside churches and restaurants, and the combination is magic. I'm there again.

And what a pleasure it was to go back to one of the most beautiful English cities I have ever visited. It wasn't in December, but I could so imagine how much the delights of the Christmas decorations or a flurry of snow would add to the charms of York.

Throw in the dramas of the world inside a hospital and the heartfelt romance between people who work there, and that's a recipe for a bit of extra seasonal joy. What could be better? How 'bout a whole series of them?

Welcome to the Royal York Hospital and, to begin, Noa and Eva's story.

Happy reading!

With love,

Alison xxx

Alison Roberts has been lucky enough to live in the South of France for several years recently but is now back in her home country of New Zealand. She is also lucky enough to write for the Harlequin Medical Romance line. A primary school teacher in a former life, she later became a qualified paramedic. She loves to travel and dance, drink champagne, and spend time with her daughter and her friends. Alison Roberts is the author of over one hundred books!

Books by Alison Roberts

Harlequin Medical Romance

A Tale of Two Midwives

Falling for Her Forbidden Flatmate
Miracle Twins to Heal Them

Daredevil Doctors

Forbidden Nights with the Paramedic
Rebel Doctor's Baby Surprise

Paramedics and Pups

The Italian, His Pup and Me

Therapy Pup to Heal the Surgeon
City Vet, Country Temptation
Paramedic's Reunion in Paradise
Midwife's Three-Date Rule
Their Fake Date Rescue

Visit the Author Profile page
at Harlequin.com for more titles.

CHAPTER ONE

'ALMOST THERE…' EVA MASON stepped back, put her hands on her hips and nodded in satisfaction. 'How perfect is that?'

The nurse behind the reception desk of the Royal York Hospital's paediatric ward leaned forward to admire the Christmas tree that Eva had just finished decorating. Every branch was generously covered with brightly coloured baubles, draped with long strands of tinsel and there were looped strings of multi-coloured lights ready to start flashing with a flick of a switch.

'It's fabulous,' Bella said. 'What are you going to put on top?'

Eva didn't say anything.

'How 'bout something different this year?' Bella suggested, her tone deliberately encouraging. 'I'll bet there's an angel in that box. Or a fairy. Hey…what about a lovely big crimson bow?'

'Nope.' Eva shook her head firmly but she was hiding a smile. She knew her colleague was teasing her. Everybody knew what a traditionalist she was when it came to Christmas and some things should never be messed with. Like putting the decorations up on the first of December when nobody was going to argue it was too soon to kick off her favourite time of the year. Or what went on the top of a Christmas tree.

'You know perfectly well that it has to be a star of Bethlehem,' she added. 'And I just happen to have one right here.'

'Of course you do.'

Bella was laughing as Eva delved into the box at her feet and took out a large star caked in silver glitter. Even on tiptoe, however, she knew she couldn't quite reach far enough to fasten the star securely.

'I need something to stand on.' Eva went around the end of the desk to get into the central hub of the ward. She picked up a chair that was in front of a computer screen.

An alarm began to sound on one of the monitors near the desk. 'That's George,' Bella sighed. '*Again*. He's supposed to be on continuous monitoring until his cardiac tests tomorrow and he thinks it's a great game to keep pulling off the electrodes.' She shut off the alarm. 'I'm good at growling at six-year-olds who should know how to follow the rules.'

Eva positioned the chair beside the tree.

'Be careful...' The warning came from the ward's charge nurse, Nicole, who reached the reception area with a pile of patient notes in her arms as Eva kicked off the comfortable clogs she wore for work, picked up the silver star and climbed onto the chair.

'Don't worry,' Eva told her. 'I've done this before.'

'That's probably what Kyle said, too.' Nicole watched Eva slip the metal ring attached to the star over the top of the uppermost upright branch of the artificial tree.

'Who's Kyle?' she asked as she twisted the wire of the branch to secure the ring.

'Kyle Woodgate. He's a singer who won a talent show on TV a few years ago and he does quite a lot of appearances around York. He got invited to come and sing some carols this afternoon before they turned the lights on for our hospital tree in the foyer.'

'Oh...' Eva sighed happily as she climbed down off the stool. 'I saw them installing it and starting the decorations yesterday. It's *such* a gorgeous tree—the biggest we've ever had. I'll bet there was a huge crowd to see it start sparkling—there must be thousands of lights on it. I was going to go down to watch but it got too busy here and then it was handover and then... I thought I'd better start *our* tree or I'll never get home.' Bella missed the pointed glance thrown at her as she was walking away towards George's room. 'I can guarantee there'll be a star on the top of *that* tree.'

'That was certainly the plan...' Nicole put the stack of notes on the desk. 'Kyle was given the honour of hanging the star before he started his show. Apparently, he climbed up the ladder, reached out to put the star on and lost his balance. He grabbed hold of the tree and managed to pull the whole thing down on top of him. I'm surprised you didn't hear the crash from up here.'

Eva's jaw dropped. 'I hope he didn't hurt himself. Or our tree. That would be a *disaster*.'

'That's what everybody's calling it—"The Great Christmas Tree Disaster". Especially Kyle. He did hurt himself. He ended up more broken than the tree, I think. Apparently, he's given himself a nasty leg fracture and other injuries to his arm or hand—or both. He was lucky he was right beside the emergency department.'

'Oh, no... He's not going to forget this Christmas in a hurry, is he? I hope he'll be okay.' Eva bit her lip, putting her shoes back on. 'Um...is the Christmas tree going to be okay?'

'It's been put back up but there's a fence around it until they can make sure it's totally secure.' Nicole sighed. 'Can you imagine how much paperwork someone in management is going to have to fill out?' She picked up the top set of patient notes from the pile. 'Speaking of paperwork, do you know where Dr Jones is at the moment? He made an urgent request for Isla Redding's notes that came in at the same time I ducked into Medical Records myself.'

'He's in with her now, getting her IV antibiotics set up. She's in Room One,' Eva said. 'She's been admitted with a nasty chest infection, poor love.'

'That's not good news.' Nicole picked up the thickest file on the desk. 'Infection's a real worry with any cystic fibrosis patient but with her underlying issues, she'll be lucky if she gets home for Christmas.'

'I'll take the notes,' Eva offered. 'I'm about to do the rounds to let kids pick a special decoration for their beds and Isla's first on my list.' She lowered her voice to a stage whisper. 'Don't tell anyone but she's my favourite patient.'

Nicole gave a huff of laughter. 'They're all your favourites, Eva.' She put Isla's notes on top of the box Eva had in her arms but shook her head. 'Isn't it time you went home?'

'Not today. It's the first of December.' Eva threw a smile over her shoulder. 'It's officially *Christmas* time and I have things to do.'

Isla looked far younger than her twelve years. She was also looking very unwell when Eva slipped quietly into one of the single rooms that had en-suite bathrooms. This room also had the best view—straight over the River Ouse to the greenery of the Museum Gardens which, for Eva, was one of the best-loved jewels in York's crown. At this time of the year, when it was dark, Isla would be able to see the magic of so many lights in the central city not far away, on the trees lining the walk bordering the gardens and on most of the riverboats moored along the edge of the river—another feature of York that Eva had missed when she'd moved to London for her first nursing position.

Okay, it had made her feel grown-up and it had been exciting for a while, especially after she'd been swept up in a whirlwind romance with Aaron who was also in his first year, training to become an anaesthetist, but the new direction in life hadn't delivered on its initial promise.

Sadly, neither had her marriage. Coming home to her family and the city she'd grown up in a few years ago now had been the first light at the end of a very dark tunnel. Shifting to work in Paediatrics instead of an emergency department more recently had been an even more inspired decision. She had the chance to get to know and love her patients, especially the chronically ill children who had frequent hospital admissions, like Isla—who really *was* one of her absolute favourites.

'Hi, sweetheart.'

'Eva…' Isla's voice was muffled beneath the oxygen mask on her face but her smile was easy to see.

Isla's mother, Kay, was hanging some clothes in a cupboard beside the bathroom. 'Eva! We were so hoping that it would be you on duty.'

'I've actually finished for today.' Eva's tone was apologetic. 'But I'll be back bright and early tomorrow to look after you, Isla. I've just popped in because Dr Noa needs these.' She lifted the heavy patient file off the top of the box after she put it down. 'They've written a whole book about you, haven't they?'

Noa Jones was on the other side of the bed. He'd noticed Eva coming into the room but hadn't let it interfere with his focus on the IV infusion that had been set up. He was watching the fluid drip into the clear chamber between the bag and the tubing that went into Isla's arm, his fingers making delicate adjustments with the little wheel to get the drip rate exactly right. Satisfied, he turned to take the notes from Eva.

'Thank you.' He flipped them open and Eva could see he was going straight to a sheaf of laboratory results. Checking what the most recent outpatient tests could tell him about her liver and kidney function, perhaps? He was frowning at the moment but he always did look kind of intense, didn't he? Totally gorgeous—but just a little bit intimidating.

You'd think he was quite fierce, in fact, until you got to know him.

Maybe it was his Pasifika heritage. Noa was a big man, tall and broad with richly dark olive skin, a flop of jet-black hair and an intriguing Polynesian style of tattoo with intricately patterned shapes like the tips of fern fronds on one arm and shoulder, the edges of which could often be glimpsed when he was wearing scrubs.

You'd think he'd be more than a little intimidating to the children he worked with but every single one of them, from tiny babies to the teenagers who were on the verge of being too old to be considered paediatric absolutely adored him.

Perhaps it was because of the way he could make his small patients, and their families, think they were the most important part of his day. Or maybe it was simply due to that smile—the one that could light up a whole room—because the joy it could encompass was just as intense as that fierceness.

He was an exceptionally attractive man but there was something about him that felt…untouchable? Aloof? No, that wasn't the right word. Aloof suggested someone was cool or disinterested and Noa was neither. There was just a distance being carefully maintained. Barriers that made it clear there were areas of his life where visitors were not welcome. The personal areas. It reminded Eva of the posters she'd put up in her bedroom as a teenager, of the pop idols she might have a major crush on but she knew they were so far away from her normal life that they might as well inhabit a different planet.

Eva had been working with Noa for more than a year now but she didn't feel as if she knew him that well. Nobody did. When he was at work, he was totally focused on his patients. When he wasn't at work, he was, presumably, just as passionate about being a single father to his gorgeous little boy, Robin. Eva had been delighted to look after the adorable three-year-old on more than one occasion, when Noa had had to bring him into work on a Saturday morning to do a ward round, but his private life was exactly that.

Private.

Eva knew better than to try crossing personal boundaries that were always there for a good reason. There were things in her own life she much preferred to keep to herself and it was a respect she was more than happy to offer her colleague.

Isla was frowning almost as fiercely as her doctor at the moment and that gave Eva a hard squeeze on her heart.

'I'm not going home just yet,' she said. 'I've got an important job to do and you're first on the list.'

She could see that Isla's rate of breathing was too rapid. So was her heart rate. The monitor screen also had the reading for the amount of oxygen in her blood that was being measured by the clip on her finger and that was too low. It was hard enough to live with a chronic illness without having it exacerbated by a complication like infection. To have it happen right before Christmas was heartbreaking.

'See this box?' Eva put it on the end of Isla's bed. 'It's full of Christmas decorations and you get first choice for something special to go on your bed—just for you.'

'What a nice idea.' Kay came to peer in the box. 'I can bring some from home, too. We were going to put *our* Christmas tree up today but it didn't quite happen. Look, Isla…there's a Santa hat in here, with shiny red sequins all over it. That might look good on top of the IV pole where it would catch all the light.'

Noa glanced up. 'Maybe somewhere else? It's better to see when a bag needs changing before the alarms start going off.'

Isla was shaking her head. 'I don't want…a Santa hat.'

Eva moved the box closer. 'You get to choose,' she said. 'Anything you like.'

Isla dug into the box as Noa spoke to Kay.

'We're starting Isla on two different antibiotics,' he told her. 'And, like last time, we'll juggle the medications if we need to when we get the results of the blood cultures that can identify exactly what we're dealing with.'

'Ooh…' Isla's mask became opaque with her breath. 'The reindeer's cute.' She lifted out a soft toy reindeer with antlers and a bell around its neck but put it down beside her to see what else was in the box. She wasn't paying any attention to the conversation between her doctor and her mother.

'She'll have twice daily physio sessions and we'll add some nebulised treatment if that's indicated and we will, of course, monitor her very closely—her oximetry, with an arterial line if that becomes necessary, her ECG, blood sugars, weight…you know the drill.'

The sincerity of the sympathy in Noa's voice was compelling enough to draw Eva's gaze towards him. She saw Kay nodding but she was pulling tissues from the sleeve of her cardigan and turning away so that her daughter couldn't see her fighting tears.

Not that Isla was looking at them. Her eyes

were wide as she pulled another decoration from the box.

'It's an angel,' she said. 'Oh…she's *so* beautiful!'

The angel had a golden dress and a halo above a little cloud of blonde curls. She also had wings that were sprinkled with gold glitter and had an attachment between them that meant she would look like she was flying when she was hung on a tree.

Or an IV pole?

'Why don't I go and find another IV pole,' Eva suggested. 'We could put it on the other side of your bed by your pillow and, that way, the angel can fly over you—day and night—and help look after you.'

'Oh…' Isla's mask was too cloudy to see her smile but her eyes were crinkling. 'Yes, *please*…'

'I'll see if I can find a bit of gold tinsel to wrap around the pole as well. I'll be right back.'

Eva found a pole in the supply room and pinched a strand of tinsel from the tree beside the reception desk. As she turned to go back to Isla's room, she almost bumped into Noa Jones who was moving fast towards the swing doors that were the entrance—and exit—to this ward.

'Sorry!' She had to step out of his way in a hurry to avoid a collision.

But Noa didn't seem to hear her.

Or see her.

And the look on his face sent a chill down Eva's spine.

She'd never seen this highly respected, incredibly skilled and totally professional doctor look anything like this. As if…

Eva caught her breath, staring at Noa's back as the doors swung back to make him disappear…

As if he could see something that absolutely terrified him?

Blinking, she turned back again and coming towards her was someone she knew from her time working in the emergency department but she wouldn't have expected to see in the ward.

'Ruby! What on earth are you doing up here?' Had her friend come to find her, perhaps, to suggest a drink after work to celebrate the start of the Christmas season?

'Can't stop,' Ruby said. 'I just came up to find Noa. It wasn't news I could pass on over the phone.'

Eva felt another shiver kiss her skin. 'What's happened?'

'It's his son,' Ruby said. 'Robin. He's being brought in by ambulance. He's had a seizure at school, either before or after he fell off a climbing frame in the playground. I've got to get back…' She looked over her shoulder as she sped past Eva. 'Call you soon.'

Eva couldn't move for a moment. A seizure? How old was Noa's little boy? Nearly four now? A head injury could cause a seizure but surely a playground at a nursery school would have a padded surface beneath climbing equipment. Was Robin epileptic? Or was this the first sign of a serious illness or something even more frightening like a brain tumour?

No wonder Noa had looked so terrified. She might not know him that well but his fear had been palpable. He'd looked as though the threat of the world ending was hanging over him. She might not be a mother herself but she was more than able to tap into the depth of love between a parent and child. Maybe the bond between a single parent and an only child was as deep as it could possibly be?

Eva glanced down at the tinsel dangling from her hand and pushed herself to start moving again. She needed to go and install Isla's angel and then she had to go right round the ward to let other children choose a decoration for their beds or walls. It might take some time but that was a good thing.

It could take them a while to do the initial assessment in the emergency department if things like X-rays or scans were ordered, but if Robin was going to be admitted to the paediatric ward she wanted to be here. She'd seen him more than once when he'd come in with his dad and maybe he would remember all the fun they'd had in the playroom the times she'd looked after him so she would be a familiar face, which could make all the difference for a frightened, unwell child.

If he didn't turn up in this ward and she hadn't heard anything by the time she was finished with her task, Eva was going to go down to the emergency department. Hopefully, it would mean he'd been discharged to go home, but Eva's instinct told her that might be wishful thinking and the haunting echo of what she'd seen on Noa's face meant there was no way she could go home herself until she knew what was happening with his son.

An emergency department was the last place that Noa Jones wanted to be.

The emergency department of the Royal York Hospital was *absolutely* the last place he wanted to be.

Especially today. When that damn Christmas tree had gone up in the foyer to signal the start of a time of the year when the memories of what had happened in this hospital almost four years ago were ready to ambush him at every turn.

To be summoned because the most important person in the world to him was arriving as a patient was…

…well, it was unthinkable, that was what it was.

Noa had stepped into a living nightmare that didn't get any better when he saw the small shape of his son being wheeled through the doors of the ambulance bay and directed swiftly to one of the fully-equipped resuscitation areas.

He actually froze for a heartbeat as he realised that Robin was being taken into the very room he'd been born in nearly four years ago, but he had to slam the door on those horrific memories.

He had to be strong.

For his son.

The person he loved more than life itself.

He was right beside Robin when the paramedic crew transferred their small patient gently to the bed and his eyelids fluttered open. His face was so pale that his eyes looked as black as the slightly-too-long waves of his hair.

'Daddy…' His voice was frightened. 'My head hurts…'

'I know, monkey. It's okay.' Noa stroked the still baby-soft skin of Robin's cheek. 'The doctors and nurses are going to look after you and I'm right here.'

'I want to go home…' A single tear escaped and rolled down to catch on Noa's finger.

'I know. Soon…' But Noa's heart broke a little as he acknowledged he couldn't make a promise like that when the reality might be very different. 'As soon as we can,' he amended.

Members of the team were getting a set of baseline vital signs. Robin clung to Noa's hand as electrodes were stuck onto his skin and an oxygen saturation clip went onto his finger. A patch that would numb the skin with local anaesthetic was placed on the back of his hand to be ready for IV access to take blood samples and deliver any medications needed. The monitor screen flashed into life with an ECG tracing and other recordings as the handover was still happening.

'He was found in a full tonic-clonic seizure on the ground beneath a climbing frame,' a paramedic reported.

'What kind of surface?' Ares Petrides, one of the A&E consultants, was leading the trauma team. 'And what height was the frame?'

'It was an aluminium climbing frame with netting and a horizontal ladder. Maximum height of around one metre and rubber tiles underneath. No obvious head injuries.'

'How long was the seizure?'

'Apparently several minutes. He was post-ictal when we arrived. Very confused and asking for his dad.'

Noa's heart broke a little more.

Ares was starting his own primary survey as

he talked to the paramedics and a scribe was recording his findings.

'Airway clear, breathing well.' Another consultant, who was in charge of airway management, smiled down at Robin. 'Can I put my stethoscope on your chest, Robin? Can you put the frog on the right place for me?'

The disc of the stethoscope had a plastic frog on the back but Robin didn't want to help it hop from one side of his chest to the other. Ares clicked on his pen torch.

'Bright light,' he warned Robin. 'Can you keep your eyes open for me?'

'Good boy,' Noa whispered, close to his ear. 'You're being so brave and I'm *so* proud of you.'

But Robin's breath caught in a hiccup and the tears were flowing faster. 'My head really hurts, Daddy.'

Ares was frowning. 'I can't say it's significant but there's a slight difference in pupil sizes.' He held up a finger. 'Can you tell me how many fingers you can see, Robin?'

It looked as though it was painful for the little boy to focus. 'One…' he finally responded, but then changed his mind. 'Two…?'

Noa's heart sank like a stone. Something serious was going on. It was hard to let go of the small hand he was holding as Ares swiftly checked the movement and strength of his limbs and hands.

'Query a slight unilateral weakness,' he said. 'We need to monitor that, too.'

'Daddy?'

'I'm here, monkey.'

'I feel sick.'

A nurse gave him a container just in time to hold for Robin.

'Let's get IV access,' Ares said. 'We need bloods off, stat and I want to get some pain relief on board. And set up for a spinal tap, please.'

Noa had to close his eyes for a moment. The chill that was running down his spine was spreading to every cell in his body.

A lumbar puncture was an invasive procedure that would only be done if the potentially fatal diagnosis of meningitis was suspected.

Robin caught sight of the needle coming towards him and shrieked in fear. '*No*... Daddy... *Daddy*...don't let them hurt me...'

But Noa was frozen again. Just for a heartbeat as a memory was forcing its way through the barriers he'd tried so hard to make impenetrable before he'd stepped into this space. It was exploding in his head and relentlessly pushing him back in time.

He could hear the continuous alarm of a monitor where the ECG line was completely flat. He could see the faces of the team as they stepped back and one of them looked up at the clock because they were about to pronounce the time of death.

He could hear the first warbling cry of his newborn son who was in the hands of the neonatal paediatric specialist who'd been part of the team to look after his wife when she'd been brought in after that terrible car accident.

He could see his wife lying on the table in this room, the wound on her belly still visible after the resuscitative hysterotomy that had been done in a desperate attempt to save the life of their unborn child after Sara had gone into cardiac arrest.

And Noa could feel the pain of his whole world shattering all over again.

CHAPTER TWO

'*Noo...*'

The frantic cry of the distressed child cut through Eva like a physical knife wound. Ruby was the first person she saw as she went past the resus room.

Robin Jones was sobbing. Struggling to pull his arm away from a nurse's touch.

'Robin knows me,' she said quietly to Ruby, having slipped into the room. 'Maybe I can help?'

Eva hadn't expected to walk into such a tense scene. She shouldn't really be here at all but she couldn't have gone home without finding out whether that fear in Noa's eyes had been justified. She'd picked up one of the leftover toys from the Christmas box, intending only to come to the emergency department and leave the toy for Robin, hopefully finding out at the same time that he was not seriously unwell.

Noa's head swivelled. '*Eva?*'

'*Eva…*' Robin was reaching out towards her.

Or was it the cuddly toy she was holding that looked like a cross between Santa Claus and an elf with a red hat and fluffy white beard, green mittens and long red and white striped legs? It didn't matter. He was distracted and his sobs were already fading to hiccups.

'Hey, sweetheart… Look—I found this lost little Santa and I think he's a bit scared. Do you think he might need a cuddle?'

People had stepped back to let Eva move right up to the bed as Robin's distress ebbed. She could feel Noa watching her. She could feel *his* distress. It had to be magnifying what was scaring this little boy, and because she wasn't so emotionally involved herself it was much easier to be calm. To smile and offer reassurance, and as Robin was clutching the toy to his chest, his head turned into Eva's hand as she stroked his hair.

It felt as if every person in the room was holding their breath. Allowing just enough time for the tension to dissipate. Eva perched on the side of the bed and found Robin wriggling right underneath her arm so that she could cuddle him the way he was now holding the toy with the long stripey legs.

She glanced up at Noa, feeling as if she should apologise for being where *he* should be, offering physical comfort to his son, but perhaps he knew that his own fear would be felt and it could make things even harder for everyone, but especially for Robin. For whatever reason, his guard was lowered and she could see gratitude in his eyes. It felt as if there was a plea there as well.

Please don't move. Please help. Robin needs you...

It felt like an invitation to step through those personal boundaries and there was no way Eva could have refused. She held his glance just long enough to make a promise that she wasn't going anywhere.

Ares nodded, as if he'd also picked up on the plea. He raised an eyebrow. 'Can you stay for a while, Eva?' he asked quietly. 'We need to do an urgent spinal tap.'

'Of course,' Eva murmured. She pressed her cheek against Robin's hair. 'Can you cuddle Santa with just one hand, sweetheart? The doctor wants to put a tiny needle in your other hand. There's special cream on it already so it won't hurt. Can you show Santa how brave you are?'

Robin burrowed his head deeper under her arm, but a moment later he uncurled one arm and held his hand out to the registrar waiting to insert a cannula. Eva's heart squeezed with something that felt like pride at this show of courage and she cuddled him closer.

The cannula was slipped into place and bandaged securely. Bloods were taken for testing and a bag of fluids hung to keep the line open. Some pain relief was administered and Eva could feel the child relaxing in her arms. Robin was almost asleep as they positioned him to take the sample of spinal fluid that would tell them if they were dealing with meningitis, where it was critical to get a diagnosis as soon as possible, but Eva didn't relax herself. She stayed right beside the little boy, holding him to make sure he didn't move as he lay on his side, his knees tucked up and his head bent down to curl his back. She kept her head close to his and talked softly the whole time, keeping him distracted if it looked like he was waking up.

'Have you written a letter to Santa, sweetheart? To tell him what you want for Christmas?'

'Noo…' The response was no more than a sleepy mumble.

'Do you know what you want?'

'Mmm…'

'What is it?'

'A puppy…'

Oops. Eva glanced up in time to catch the way Noa closed his eyes—as if he'd heard this request too many times and it was a no-go. Because of the usual Christmas campaign that reminded people that puppies were forever and not just for Christmas? Or was it that a needy pet would

tip the balance for a single parent when it was
hard enough to cope anyway? She might need
to apologise later, although it seemed unlikely
that Robin was going to remember as he drifted
into a deeper sleep.

Antibiotics were started as soon as the fluid
sample had been taken, even though the diagnosis had not been confirmed and there were no
signs of any rash yet.

Robin was roused so that neurological checks
could be repeated and this time, after his pupils
were checked for reaction to light, Ares caught
Noa's gaze, his face very serious.

'They're significantly different in size and reaction now,' he said. 'And that right-sided weakness is more pronounced. We need to rule out a
brain bleed.'

'X-ray?' Noa's voice was hollow. 'CT scan?'

'An MRI would be more definitive,' Ares said.
'And we don't have any time to waste.'

Eva knew they would have to sedate Robin
completely to put him into the MRI machine so
there was no real reason for her to stay.

But she couldn't leave. She was part of this
medical drama that was playing out. She needed
to know what was going on. She would really
like to be here when Robin woke up again, but
in the meantime she knew that—whether he was

aware of it or not—Noa needed a friend. Someone who was here for *him*, as well as his son.

And she wanted that person to be her.

Because she didn't want to go home until she
knew whether Robin was going to be okay.

Because she knew what it was like to be alone
when it felt as if your world might be crumbling
around you and just having someone there for
no other reason than to offer support could have
made such a difference?

Or was it because she'd seen that fear in Noa's
eyes?

And it felt as if she'd seen right through those
walls he kept around his private life—and himself.

The passing of time became irrelevant.

Things seemed to take forever, as if the world
had slowed down its normal orbit, yet so much
was happening at speed around him. Noa was
desperate for the dots to be joined, a diagnosis
made and whatever treatment his son needed to
be initiated, but when it finally happened all he
wanted to do was to turn the clock back. To reset
his world so that none of this was happening.

The Royal York Hospital's best doctors in
every field were gathering to support their colleague. The way they always had, ever since the
terrible moments of Robin's birth. They'd cov-

ered for him to try and help in those early months of struggling to cope. They'd held his job open and welcomed him back. They had become his professional family when he was too numb from tragedy to even consider the upheaval of moving countries again to be closer to his parents. Then the hospital creche had become a second home for Robin until he was old enough for nursery school, so the bonds became tighter. The people here genuinely cared about them and that had made it a good place to be.

It didn't feel like a place he wanted to be right now, however.

The head of Radiology was right by his side as the images from the MRI filled the screens around them and Noa could see from his expression that the news wasn't going to be good.

'There you go…right there… See that isointense ring? It's a brain abscess. Has Robin been unwell in the last two or three weeks?'

'Yes. He had a course of antibiotics for an ear infection. But that's at least two weeks ago. I thought he was well over it.'

It was the paediatric ICU physician who picked up the significant deterioration in Robin's condition as his confusion and nausea increased.

That was when the world darkened around Noa. You couldn't let pressure rise too high inside the closed space of a skull. Because that meant there was an increasing risk of brain herniation, which was highly likely to be fatal. Not that anyone was saying that out loud, but the speed with which the paediatric neurosurgeon put the wheels into motion for emergency surgery was impressive.

'We'll do a simple aspiration,' he told Noa. 'A burr hole that will give us access to drain the abscess. Then we'll keep him in ICU on antibiotics and monitor with CT scans to make sure he's responding. This surgery will take about an hour. Have you got someone to stay with you while you wait?'

Noa shook his head. 'I'm fine.'

He didn't find out that he was wrong on both counts until they stopped Robin's bed at the entrance to the suite of operating theatres on the first floor of the hospital. Beside the room where relatives were allowed to wait. In front of the swing doors with the big notice above saying entry was only for authorised personnel.

Robin was still sound asleep from the sedation for the MRI so there was no need for Noa to be there while the anaesthetist prepared him for the surgery. There was no need for the comfort of that strange Santa toy with the striped legs either, though Noa didn't understand why Eva had come all this way, a short time ago, to take charge of the toy.

He smoothed back Robin's hair and placed a soft kiss on his son's forehead.

'See you soon, monkey,' he whispered. 'I love you...'

It was seeing the bed disappear through those doors that did him in. Noa was holding back tears as he finally turned to go and count every second of the next hour in that relatives' room because that was as close as he was allowed to be.

He wasn't fine at all.

But he also wasn't alone.

He went into the relatives' room to find Eva sitting on one of the small couches, the red and white toy on her lap.

'You don't have to stay,' he said. 'I can make sure Robin gets the toy when he wakes up again.'

'I want to stay,' she said quietly. 'And it's not about the toy. I can't go home knowing that you'd be waiting here by yourself.'

Noa opened his mouth to say that he'd coped alone for years now. He preferred to face things alone because that meant he could continue to cope, as he had done since his world had imploded on the day Robin was born. But how could he dismiss the kindness he was being shown by someone he might not know on a personal basis but he knew what a great nurse she was? How compassionate and genuinely caring she was with all her patients.

It had been Eva who'd broken Robin's spiralling fear and that heartrending crying. He couldn't begin to tell her how grateful he'd been for that and he certainly couldn't tell her to go home either. So Noa didn't say anything. He gave a single nod, sat down on the other couch and put his face in his hands.

Eva didn't break the silence as many people might have done, to offer platitudes or unfounded hope. She seemed to be content to simply be there so he wasn't alone. A human presence that did, in fact, offer a surprising level of comfort because it stopped him forgetting where he was and sinking too far into that dark space that was way too close.

It was so quiet in this waiting room that the clock could be heard, the minutes ticking by far more slowly than seemed possible.

Eva was tempted to break the silence but instinct told her that it would break what felt like an oddly solid bond. More than once, she let her gaze slip sideways to rest on Noa, and when she wasn't looking, she was thinking about him and what they had in common.

They both worked in the same area of the hospital, presumably because they both loved working with children.

He was about her age, she guessed—in his mid-thirties.

They'd both been married. Eva didn't know exactly how Noa had lost his wife, but she did know that he'd been tragically widowed and left with a baby boy to raise alone. Her own story was very different. A husband who'd cheated on her and had been very much alive when he'd finally told her that he wanted to end their marriage to be with the woman he was having a longstanding affair with. Tragedy hadn't ripped her marriage apart—she just hadn't been worth keeping as a wife.

So she and Noa were both single and seemed to share the intention of staying that way. Eva wasn't one to listen to gossip but she knew there were a lot of women who worked in this hospital who'd tried—and failed—to attract the attention of Dr Jones. Understandably. He was not only a highly respected doctor but he was astonishingly good-looking and there was something absolutely heart-melting about a single dad, wasn't there? Knowing that a man was capable of nurturing a child on his own.

Eva *had* wanted to fill that gap but even a hesitant attempt at online dating had confirmed that the scars of being such a failure were too deep to get past. She was starting to realise how much happier she was on her own.

The clock kept ticking but Eva still didn't say anything. She was still lost in thought.

There were bigger things they didn't have in common.

Eva was a Yorkie, born and raised here in York and proud of her ties to one of England's most beautiful historic cities. It was always very obvious that Noa had his roots on some sun-kissed Pacific Island on the other side of the world. But, even more significantly, Noa was a father.

Eva had tried—and failed—to become a mother for years. She was finally at peace with the knowledge that she would never have children of her own, but that didn't mean she couldn't imagine what Noa must be going through right now. How it must feel as if his own heart had been ripped out and was lying on the operating table with his son.

She didn't realise that her breath had been released in an audible sigh until she felt Noa's gaze on her as he raised his head.

She turned and for a heartbeat—and then another—she held his gaze. She should say something, for both their sakes, she decided. Sitting here in such a heavy silence was probably making them both too aware of what was happening in that theatre.

It was Noa who broke the silence.

'What's with the weird stockings that Santa's got on? Isn't he supposed to have red trousers that match his jacket?'

'I know, right?' Eva held the toy up. 'And he's got shoes with pointy toes instead of boots.'

'They're elf legs.'

'Maybe the wrong limbs came along the assembly line. The green mittens on his hands aren't quite right either. Maybe that's why the other kids in the ward rejected him when they were choosing their special decorations.'

One side of Noa's mouth lifted in a poignant kind of half-smile. 'Robbie liked him.' It was *his* breath that came out in a sigh this time as he looked up at the clock. 'It's been nearly an hour. Shouldn't be much longer.'

'Will he come onto our ward?'

'He'll have to go into the intensive care unit first. They'll be watching his ICP like hawks. If draining the abscess isn't enough, he'll have to go back and have more surgery.' His voice was quieter now, as if he was voicing his own fears aloud. 'They'd have to do a craniotomy in that case and remove a portion of his skull to gain access to completely remove the abscess.' Noa cleared his throat. 'He will come up to our ward at some point, though. I'm glad it's a familiar place for him and that he knows some of the staff.'

Like *her*?

Yes…there was a warmth in Noa's eyes that was recognition and Eva felt it soak in through her skin. She also felt suddenly shy.

Because Noa was seeing her? And it didn't feel like he was only seeing her as merely one of the staff. For some reason her heart rate picked up and she could feel an odd tingle skid across her skin.

Did she *want* him to notice her as more than a colleague?

No, her head told her.

But it felt as if her body was whispering *yes*.

She was trying to think of something to say that didn't risk making this moment more significant than it had been intended to be when the paediatric neurosurgeon appeared at the door and Noa's attention shifted with the speed of a laser beam.

'It went well,' the surgeon said. 'Intracranial pressure's dropping and we've got a sample off to identify exactly what bug we're dealing with. He's in Recovery if you'd like to come and sit with him?'

Noa was already on his feet. He began to walk out of the room without a backward glance, but maybe he caught Eva's movement from the cor-

ner of his eye as she also got to her feet and held
out the toy.

She didn't need to say anything.

And it was time she went home.

For the second time today, as she stepped
out of the room, she watched Noa's back as he
walked through a set of swing doors and was
about to vanish. The big, powerful man was
holding the Santa toy by one of his green mittens and the long striped legs were dangling.

It brought tears to Eva's eyes.

And a wobbly smile to her lips.

The remnants of that whisper in her body
could still be heard.

CHAPTER THREE

NORMAL LIFE FOR Noa Jones had come to a shockingly abrupt halt the moment he'd heard that his son was on his way to hospital in an ambulance.

The hours between his arrival in the emergency department and his admission to the paediatric intensive care unit were a blur of urgent treatment, too many people and potentially life-or-death decisions to be made.

After his surgery and time in Recovery, when Robin was settled into the glass box that was his private space in the intensive care unit, the entire world became what was happening in this room and as that first interminable night morphed into a new day, the only reason Noa moved away from Robin's bedside was for the quickest bathroom break possible. There was a reclining chair in the corner of the room but he didn't even try and sleep that first night. There were half a dozen monitors crowded around the bed, with information in the constantly fluctuating numbers, the soft beep of a heart rate and rhythm and alarms that sounded when set parameters were breached and Noa was doing his best to watch every single one of them. It almost felt as if the moment he stopped being vigilant enough, something horrible might happen.

Robin was deeply unconscious in an induced coma, his airway and breathing being managed by a ventilator and the pressure inside his head being monitored closely by a thin probe that went through a hole that had been drilled into his skull. He had electrodes dotted on his scalp and stuck to his chest, IV lines that were delivering high doses of antibiotics and countless wires and tubes that were carefully sorted but still looked like technological spaghetti.

The ICU nurses and doctors, along with technicians and therapists, came and went quietly and Noa clung to the words of reassurance that they were happy with the condition of his precious son. He silenced the questions that his brain tried to throw at him—the 'what-if's and endless possible complications that could be lurking around the next corner—because he wasn't Robin's doctor. Right now, he was simply a father and the only member of his very small family who was close enough to be able to offer the love and support that this little boy needed.

It could have been horribly lonely but Noa was used to being a solo parent and dealing with whatever came his way. Being able to call his parents was a comfort and, astonishingly, so was that strange Santa-elf toy that was propped at the end of Robin's bed. It reminded him that the entire world hadn't stopped. That Christmas was coming and he had to hang onto the hope that Robin would have recovered enough to be able to enjoy the treats of the happy family day he was looking forward to so much this year because his grandparents were coming all the way across the world from New Zealand for the occasion.

What felt even bigger than that, however, was the reminder that Noa hadn't been alone in what had been the scariest time so far—when he'd been waiting for his child to get through the surgery on his brain.

Eva Mason, the gentle, efficient and popular nurse from his ward had, for whatever reason, chosen to stay by his side. To breathe the same air and become invested in the outcome of the turmoil his life had so unexpectedly dropped into. Had he thanked her properly? It was an amazing thing to do for someone who wasn't family or a close friend. They were nothing more than colleagues really, given the way he deliberately protected a private life that was centred purely on himself and his son, so it was a glimpse of what made Eva who she was.

And she had a heart as big as Africa. A compassion that was bone-deep and a love of children that was as genuine as she was. She was, quite simply, a lovely person.

Noa didn't let people get too close but it felt as if Eva had quietly slipped into a space that was rather a lot more than simply a colleague. Not that he was going to try and put any label on what that space was because even his friends were kept at a safe distance and nobody could get closer than a friend.

It did feel as if it *could* be closer, though, which was the best reason not to try and analyse it.

He had far more important things on his mind right now and it was easy to let other thoughts evaporate. This was nothing to be concerned about because it also felt, curiously, as if Eva belonged in whatever space she'd entered. He didn't need to usher her out and make sure the door was firmly closed behind her.

Eva didn't normally stop at the small café near the Royal York Hospital that was renowned for the best coffee for miles, but she ducked in on her way to work today and ordered a takeaway drink and a delicious-looking toasted bacon sandwich.

The coffee was still hot when she entered the paediatric intensive care unit that was close enough to be on her way to her ward. She found the night shift staff gathering at the central hub of the reception area, preparing for handover.

'Can I leave this here for Noa Jones?' she asked. 'I had a feeling he might not be wanting to go as far as it took to find any breakfast.'

'Take it in,' a nurse said with a smile as she looked up from the notes she was writing. 'He's in Room Two, right behind you.'

Eva turned. The rooms, with their clear glass walls, were set in a square around this central area and, yes…in the room closest to where she was standing, she could see Noa sitting beside a bed, his shoulders hunched as he leaned forward far enough to have his hand resting on the pillow, his fingers against Robin's cheek.

'How is he?' she asked. 'Has he had any sleep?'

The nurse shook her head. 'Not a wink. I expect he'll be grateful for that coffee.' With another smile, she went back to the notes she clearly needed to finish before handover and Eva knew she was disrupting their routine.

She took a deep breath, pushed aside a wave of something like shyness at disturbing Noa, and went to the door of Room Two. She held up the takeaway coffee cup with its lid and the paper bag with the bacon sandwich as she poked her head around the door.

'I thought of you as I passed the café,' she said

softly. 'I know you probably won't feel like eating, but it *is* important.'

Oh, *my*...

Noa looked wrecked. His hair was a rumpled mess and the lines around his eyes were deeper than Eva had ever seen them. Oddly, it made him more attractive than ever. So much so that Eva felt an odd internal thump—as though someone had nudged her with a very sharp elbow in order to wake her up.

He was also clearly exhausted but the aura of determination to keep going was palpable. So was the love he had for his son and that was... heartbreakingly admirable.

Noa drew in an appreciative breath through his nose. 'Is that coffee I can smell? And *bacon*?'

'I didn't know what you'd like. It's just a strong flat white. No sugar. And I figured everyone likes bacon.'

'Perfect. Thank you.' It looked as though it took an effort for Noa to break the physical contact he had with Robin so that he could move to take the coffee cup.

Eva's gaze scanned the monitors and then settled on Robin's face and she could feel her face tightening in response to the squeeze on her heart—as if she was trying to make sure she didn't show too much concern—or worse—blink back tears at the sight of his little face half-hidden by the tubing of the ventilator. She knew that Noa was watching her reaction.

'He's doing well,' he said. 'They want to keep him sedated and on the ventilator for twenty-four hours—maybe longer—but things are stable.'

Eva let out a breath she hadn't realised she was holding.

'If there's anything I can do, just ask, won't you?'

'We'll be fine,' Noa said.

'Let me leave you my phone number, just in case.' Eva bit her lip as she pulled a notepad and pen from her pocket. 'I could sit with Robin for a bit, if you wanted to get home and collect anything for him?' She glanced at the lonely Santa toy on the end of the bed as she finished scribbling her number. 'Like a favourite toy or blanket or something, for when he wakes up?'

Noa nodded but his gaze was already back on Robin and Eva wasn't sure he had even heard her offer. She slipped away as quietly as she'd arrived. It was time to start her shift and she knew there was a little girl with an angel above her bed who would be waiting for her arrival.

It was almost a surprise to see the lights on the Christmas tree beside the reception desk in the paediatric ward twinkling as she arrived.

Had it only been yesterday that she'd climbed

up to fasten the star on the top to begin celebrating the start of this joyous season? She'd stuck the string of gingerbread people holding hands along the front of the desk too, so that the colourful decoration could welcome the staff, visitors and especially the children who were, after all, the focus of this place that she loved to work in so much.

Isla was one of the patients assigned to Eva that day and she spent a lot of time in her room, keeping a careful watch on her condition, encouraging her to eat and drink a little and helping with the intensive physiotherapy sessions that were vital to improve her breathing and deliver more oxygen to her body as it battled the infection. Physiotherapists were visiting twice a day and Eva set up the nebuliser to administer a hypertonic saline solution that Isla could inhale before her sessions that would help shift the mucus clogging her lungs—along with the percussion that the physios or Kay would perform on her chest—to make it easier for her to try and clear her airways by coughing.

Little Robin Jones was never far from her mind, especially when she was getting five-year-old Oscar prepared to go to Theatre to get his appendix removed. His mother's anxiety was contagious and the sedation Eva had administered was going to take some time to be effective. He was clinging to his mother and sobbing.

'You're very lucky, Oscar,' Eva told him.

'Why?'

'Because it's December and you're the first person to get a ride in the special Christmas bed that's only for boys and girls who are going to have an operation.'

Oscar still had tears rolling down his cheeks but there was a spark of interest in his eyes.

'What sort of bed?'

'It's a Christmas sleigh,' Eva said. 'You know, the sort that gets pulled by Rudolph the Red-Nosed Reindeer? It's red and gold and sparkly.'

During any other month of the year, children could choose between a racing car or a princess carriage for their transport to Theatre but, years ago, a hospital handyman had created Christmas sleigh sides to attach to a hospital bed and the tradition had expanded so that the porter pushing the bed had a role to play as well. They always wore some reindeer antlers or a Santa hat and as it got closer to Christmas Day they could often be heard singing a carol or two.

'The reindeer aren't allowed in the hospital,' Eva said sadly, 'but the bed has red sheets. And bells that jingle. Listen… I think I can hear it coming… Are you ready for your ride?'

Oscar had stopped crying completely now. He was almost smiling.

'Can Mummy come too?'

'Of course she can. She might even be allowed to ride on the bed with you.'

Oscar's mother was looking a lot happier as well. It was no problem for her to be on the bed with her son, cuddling him as they were whisked away on the sleigh. Eva went with them and she was beaming when she got back to the ward.

'I love the Christmas bed,' she announced, pausing for just a moment to soak in the pleasure of the coloured lights winking on the tree beside the central hub of the paediatric ward. 'I love the way it makes everybody smile and wave as it goes past.'

Bella was printing off an ECG trace. Ward rounds were about to start and a paediatric cardiologist was coming to review George and would probably schedule an exercise test for later today to see if there were any significant changes from his resting heart rhythm that might explain the fainting episodes that had led to his admission.

As the hours sped past in a busy shift, Eva gave up expecting that Noa would ask her for any assistance. Why would he? There was nothing special about her. She was simply another nurse amongst many that he worked with. When her phone buzzed in her pocket late that afternoon when she was getting ready to go home, she was surprised to find a message from a number she didn't recognise.

She was even more surprised to find that the message had come from Noa.

Her heart sank but then sped up as she read the message.

If your offer's still open, it would be great if you could sit with Robin for a bit. I need to get home for a shower and a change of clothes etc. I know he's not conscious but I'd feel better if someone he knows was here with him.

Eva's thumbs moved swiftly.

Perfect timing. My shift is almost done. Be there asap.

She added a smiley face but then deleted it. This couldn't be a more serious time in Noa's life. The frivolity of emojis might feel like a slap in the face.

The charge nurse, Nicole, was only too happy to let Eva go a little early when she heard that Noa needed her help.

'I think he's going to dash home to get a shower and some fresh clothes. Probably some things for Robin too, for when he wakes up.'

'Tell him we're all thinking of them both,'

Nicole said. 'And he doesn't need to worry about any work-related issues. Everything's under control and his surgical lists and inpatients are all covered. He can be with Robin for as long as he needs to be.'

Eva sat in the comfortable chair right beside Robin's bed when she took over Noa's vigil.

'Take as long as you like,' she told him. 'I've got your number so I can let you know if anything changes. Try and eat something if you can. I don't have to get home for anything so you could get a bit of sleep, even? It can't be easy to get more than a few minutes at a time in here.'

'That chair's fine.' Noa's voice was dismissive—as if sleep was the last thing he was worried about. 'I shouldn't be more than an hour or so. Thanks for this, Eva.'

The hint of a smile on his face made Eva feel grateful for the opportunity she'd been given to help. She suspected that asking for any kind of help wasn't something that was normal for this proud man.

She wasn't alone in the room to begin with. A nurse came and went quietly, recording vital signs on a chart, printing out a strip of an ECG trace and, at one point, hanging a new bag of IV fluids that had a bright orange medication label stuck to it, probably for the high-dose antibiotics it contained. A senior respiratory therapist, who'd been working with Isla only that morning, came to check on the ventilator settings and equipment. If he was surprised to see Eva there, he covered it well. Both Robin's neurosurgeon and an ICU consultant popped in briefly. They didn't discuss their patient's progress in the room but Eva could read their body language and the look they exchanged. They were happy with how things were going.

Eva found she could relax more, then. She curled up in the chair and rested her elbow on the side of Robin's bed, her hand holding his gently, her thumb rubbing his palm. She could feel the squishiness of the cushioning in this chair. When the leg support was raised, it was probably quite comfortable to sleep in for a parent that didn't want to leave their child's side.

Like Noa. If he'd slept at all, it would have been in this chair. When she was finally left alone with Robin and she found her mind drifting as she listened to the hypnotic beeping of the monitors, she could imagine Noa in this chair, so tired he couldn't keep his eyes open but still holding his son's hand. She could actually feel that love for his son and it woke something that had been dormant in her own heart for a long time now.

Or maybe it was the sensation of those small fingers she was holding right now. It had been part of the dream, hadn't it? To have and to hold a small hand just like this. To play with the fingers of a newborn baby and marvel at the miracle of how tiny and perfect they were. To hold the hand of a toddler as he or she started to learn to walk. To be there to comfort an older child when they were sick or frightened.

Like she was doing now.

Holding a hand and talking softly. Saying words that were reassuring. It didn't matter what they were, really, did it? If Robin could hear her on some subconscious level, it would be the tones of comfort—the song a mother instinctively sang—that he would be aware of. It was something Eva knew how to do, even if she was never going to be a mother herself.

The fierceness of that yearning to have her own child was a lot less disruptive these days, of course. Time didn't exactly heal everything but it could certainly push the mute button. Sitting here like this, though, Eva was being taken back through time to when it was all she wanted. When the evidence that she wasn't pregnant became more and more of a disappointment as each cycle came and went and months turned into a year. The worst had been when she was a day or two later than usual and hope kicked in. Not that Aaron had ever been overly affected. They had plenty of time, he said. They were probably too young for parenthood yet anyway and it was fun trying, wasn't it?

It wasn't fun when one year had turned into two. The diary-keeping had started then. And the tests. Blood tests. An ultrasound. Even a laparoscopy in the end. The decision to try IVF had sparked the biggest hope of all, but that had been derailed with devastating effect before Eva had even attended the first appointment with the clinic that they'd had to wait so long for.

She'd been the one who'd had to ring and cancel that appointment and it had been the worst phone call she'd ever made. What could she say?

Sorry, but I've just found out that my husband has been having an affair with someone who works at the same hospital we do. It's not that he doesn't love me any longer but, you know— apparently our marriage has 'lost its spark'. He thought I should know the truth before we went any further with trying to have a baby. Goodness knows how long he might have waited to tell me otherwise, but there it is. I think I'd better cancel this appointment rather than postpone it, don't you?

No. She hadn't said that. She had managed not to cry but she hadn't said much at all, really.

'I'd like to cancel the appointment, please. I've changed my mind.'

Eva hadn't been working in Paediatrics then.

It might have been unthinkable before she'd got through the first horrible months of her marriage ending—and the feeling that it was her whole life as she'd dreamed it would be as a wife and mother that had been destroyed. Leaving London to come closer to the support of her family and the joy of her sister's children had been healing. The pull towards the children that came through the emergency department had been too strong to ignore after that and the postgraduate training she'd done to become a paediatric nurse had been a whole new beginning that she had embraced wholeheartedly.

So here she was, an experienced senior nurse trusted by parents to care for the most precious thing in their lives—their children. Eva was proud of who she was and what she did. And if it meant that occasionally she would feel some personal heartbreak that it was never going to be her own child's hand that she was holding, it might actually be a good thing because she was never going to become complacent. Or forget how much this meant.

And this time something felt different.

She was in deeper than usual. She felt like a part of this little boy's story and…it felt even more important than ever to *be* a part of it, perhaps because there was such a glaring gap in the lives of Noa and Robin and she could, at least temporarily, help to fill that space in some way.

She wasn't going to let it surface but she couldn't deny the ripple of the undercurrent in how she felt that was about her rather than her patient.

About the glaring gap in *her* life?

Eva was still holding Robin's hand when Noa returned. He was wearing jeans and a clean shirt with the sleeves rolled up and she caught a whiff of the soap—or maybe it was the shampoo—he'd used very recently as he leaned past her to stroke the hair back from his son's face.

What was that scent? Something smoky. Or woodsy. Or was musky the right word?

Was it even a commercial product? The way it was curling into Eva's nostrils and then dissipating through her entire body made her wonder if she was simply breathing in something purely masculine. Goodness knows, she hadn't been close enough to a freshly showered man for so long, she'd probably forgotten.

It certainly wasn't something she should be thinking about in relation to Noa Jones, anyway. Eva hurriedly uncurled her legs and slipped out of the chair.

'I'll get out of your way,' she whispered. 'He's been absolutely fine—sleeping so peacefully.'

Noa nodded. 'I had a chat with his doctors

as I came in. They've lined up another MRI for first thing tomorrow and if that's looking good, we'll wake him up. Maybe even get him out of ICU.' He reached into a bag he'd brought back with him and took out a rather battered-looking teddy bear that he tucked into bed beside Robin. 'I couldn't find his favourite cuddly,' he said, 'Sheepy—a funny flat thing that looks like it's an empty cover for a hot-water bottle.'

'Sounds like a lovey,' Eva said.

'It's the one he's slept with since he was a baby—but this is his second favourite. I couldn't spend too long looking because I wanted to get back to him.' His gaze was holding Eva's. 'Thanks again. There's nobody else I would have asked. Robbie really likes you. More importantly, he trusts you.'

'I like him, too.' Eva smiled. 'And I can come back tomorrow if you want to go and have another look for Sheepy.'

Noa nodded again. 'He might be awake by then,' he said. 'And, yeah…sleepy Sheepy might be being missed more then so getting home for a proper hunt might be a good idea.'

'It's a date then.' Eva smiled, heading for the door. 'See you tomorrow.'

Her smile faded the instant she turned away, however, and she was kicking herself mentally—

hard—by the time she escaped the unit. Cringing, even.

What on earth had made her say *that*?

A *date*?

With Noa Jones?

She could only hope he would assume it was, as intended, a throwaway reference to an upcoming arrangement.

Of course he would, she decided as she headed into the chilly December evening.

Anything else would be…well…unthinkable.

Wouldn't it…?

CHAPTER FOUR

ROBIN JONES WAS kept in the intensive care unit for twenty-four hours after coming off life support so that his medical team could be confident that his intra-cranial pressure was not going to rise to dangerous levels again. Then he was transferred to the paediatric ward and went into the room next door to Isla's. To Noa's relief, his son was also put under the primary nursing care of Eva Mason.

Noa hadn't been able to find the missing toy sheep on another quick visit home but he had collected items like pyjamas and favourite books and some other toys so the defining edges of a hospital environment and home were beginning to blur enough to not feel like this was such an alien place to be with his son. The time spent in Eva's company was also beginning to feel familiar enough to be important. She clearly cared about his little boy enough for it to feel like Robin was the knot in the centre of a strand between Noa and Eva that they were both holding tightly at each end.

The first few days on the ward were kept as quiet as possible. Robin was still on medications for the pain of headaches and to prevent seizures, IV antibiotics and sedation to avoid overstimulation that could elevate cerebral pressure which, in turn, could lead to potentially permanent brain damage. What kind of damage might have already occurred couldn't be assessed until he was properly awake so, although it was a big step forward in his recovery to be on the ward and half-awake at times, there was still a tension that was hovering in the background like a dark cloud.

Noa had been given access to the on-call bedroom at this end of the ward if he wanted a quieter place to try and sleep rather than the reclining chair in Robin's room. He had full use of the staff facilities and he could shower and get a clean set of scrubs whenever he needed to. He could also use either the staffroom or the kitchen that was available for the parents of children in the ward to make a coffee or sandwich at any time, but they were never as good as the breakfast that was becoming a habit for Eva to pick up for him at the nearby café on her way in to work.

'Just tell me if you're getting sick of bacon sandwiches,' she said. 'They do some really good banana muffins too.'

'I can't let you do this every day, Eva. Not if you don't let me reimburse you.' He had tried, and failed, more than once to do that.

'It's a small thing,' she'd responded quietly. 'And I like to think of it as paying something forward. You never know when you might need a bit of kindness yourself.' He'd seen the quirk of her eyebrows then, as if she was deliberately trying to lighten the atmosphere. 'Besides...we both know how rubbish the coffee is here.'

Noa simply smiled. He wasn't about to complain about the coffee the hospital provided. Or the food in the cafeteria. It was irrelevant in comparison to the excellent care his son was receiving. He did make a mental note, however, to keep an eye on Eva. He'd be the first to step in at any hint that she might need a helping hand or a kind word but, even if she didn't, he would find some way of showing his appreciation for the support she was so generously providing. He could send her some flowers, perhaps. Or take her out for a really nice dinner.

Whoa...

Where had *that* thought come from?

It was just as well he was staring at Eva's back as she left to get to the shift-changeover meeting when that thought came out of nowhere.

Dinner?

Alone with Eva?

Like some kind of...*date*...?

It wasn't going to happen, of course. Okay... maybe Noa had become more aware of the lack of feminine company in his life recently, but Robin had always taken priority and this crisis, along with the fear of what challenges might lie in its aftermath, made the idea of choosing to spend time on something far too close to a dinner-date more than a little shocking.

It was unacceptable, that was what it was.

So it should be no trouble at all to forget about it completely.

Where had the first week of December gone?

The Royal York Hospital was well infused with the Christmas spirit now. More and more decorations were appearing. The huge tree in the foyer that had fallen onto the unfortunate singer, Kyle Woodgate, had passed safety inspections, the fencing was down and there were pretend gifts of brightly wrapped cardboard boxes around the base. The red sleigh bed was a regular sight between the paediatric wards and the theatre suite on the first floor and Eva Mason was not only wearing her Christmas-themed scrubs but her impressive collection of decorative headbands was in use.

Today, her headband featured small ears and reindeer antlers with sprigs of holly at the bottom like ribbons. Her scrub tunic was bright green with Christmas motifs like candy canes, bells, snowmen and…

'*Robins…*' The small boy in the bed was much more alert as his sedation was being lifted. 'There are robins on your top.'

'There are indeed.' Eva was carefully drawing blood from the catheter in his hand. The longer this small plastic tube could stay in position and patent, the better the chances of avoiding the trauma of a child being stuck with more needles than absolutely necessary.

'They're my favourite birds,' she told Robin. 'Because they're Christmas birds and I love Christmas.'

'Who would have guessed?' Noa was tidying the overbed table that was cluttered with various toys and the remains of Robin's barely tasted lunch. There was no hint of sarcasm in his tone, however. Eva caught a one-sided curl of his lips when she let her gaze flick sideways for a heartbeat. She was so used to Noa being in the room by now that she actually missed him if he took the opportunity to take a break while she was there with his son. She'd even stayed after her shift ended yesterday so he could go home and have yet another hunt for the sheep toy that was still missing.

'That's why I was called Robin, wasn't it, Daddy?'

'It was, monkey. They were your mummy's favourite birds, too. And you were supposed to be born on Christmas Day.'

'But I came early, didn't I?'

'Just by a few days,' Noa agreed. Something in his tone made Eva glance in his direction again, but he was focused on removing the lunch tray to make more room for the toys. Arriving on an expected delivery date was far less common than people realised so it would have been perfectly normal for Robin to have been born a few days before, but that note in Noa's response suggested that it might have been more than simply a surprise. Had it been alarming in some way?

She wasn't going to ask such a personal question, of course. Besides, she was distracted by making a mental note to check the actual date of Robin's birth in his notes. Birthdays were a close second to Christmas on the list of important things to celebrate. Especially for children.

'It's nearly my birthday now.' The effort of so much talking was tiring Robin out. He lay back on his pillows and watched Eva transferring the blood into the tubes that would be sent to the lab.

'It is.' Noa was carefully balancing a small robot on its feet at one end of the table.

'You're going to be four, aren't you?' Eva made sure she sounded impressed.

'Yes.' But the pride in his voice was instantly replaced by anxiety. 'Will I be better enough to go home for my birthday party, Daddy?'

'We'll see, monkey.'

There was a small silence as Eva swabbed the plug on the end of the catheter and rebandaged Robin's hand to protect the line from being knocked. She didn't try to catch Noa's gaze this time. They both knew that Robin couldn't go home while he was on the strong IV antibiotics that were capable of crossing the blood-brain barrier and in need of intensive monitoring that included regular blood tests and scans that could well need to be continued for more than another couple of weeks. Robin wouldn't even be allowed out of bed unless he had a soft helmet on to protect his head from any bumps that could happen due to the one-sided weakness in his body that this crisis had caused. Or if he had another seizure.

Eva automatically went to the next item on her routine of taking the blood test and vital signs for her patient. She turned to check the IV line that was providing his antibiotics and make sure it was running well and there were no signs of infection beneath the clear plastic covering the insertion site, but she leaned down to speak to

Robin in a whisper as she did so, as if she was imparting a secret.

'If you're still here for your birthday, we'll make sure it's the best party ever,' she promised.

Robin's eyes were closed now as he drifted back to sleep but there was a smile on his face.

There was no hint of a smile on Noa's face, though, as Eva collected the tubes to deliver to the phlebotomist who was doing her rounds on the ward. She needed to collect Isla's as well. Was he staring at her so intently because he knew she was about to leave the room?

'I'll be back in a minute,' she told him. 'And I can stay with Robin if you need to get anything done.'

She'd caught him yesterday at the nurses' station, checking notes on his patients whose care had been taken over by other doctors. There had been no choice but to be constantly by his son's side when this personal drama had started but, now that Robin was recovering, she knew that Noa was feeling the pull to get back to the job he was so passionate about.

'I don't have anything on after my shift today,' she added. 'I'm happy to stay with Robin for a few hours and read stories or watch a movie with him if…you wanted to catch up on your patients? Like George? Did you know he's been diagnosed with Long QT syndrome after an exercise stress test? Turns out there's a family history of sudden death, including an uncle who'd been diagnosed with epilepsy in his teens.'

She could see the flare of focus in Noa's eyes and the concern for the six-year-old he'd admitted himself the day Robin had fallen ill.

'It could have been misdiagnosed,' he said. 'Maybe the seizures were hypoxic due to lack of oxygen from an episode of ventricular fibrillation that self-reverted.'

'Exactly what the cardiologist suggested.' Eva found herself smiling. She would have expected nothing less in the way of diagnostic skill from a paediatric doctor who had to have far more than a basic knowledge of every specialty to do his job for the daunting variety of sick children who came under his care. 'He's being kept in for a day or two longer to see how he responds to beta blockers if you want to catch up with how he's doing.'

She hesitated, wondering if she might be stepping over a boundary that was less than professional. 'He's safe with us and you only need to be close by,' she added quietly. 'You don't need to be in this room all day and all night.'

'I'm his father,' Noa said. 'This is where I *should* be.'

'You have to look after yourself, too,' Eva said gently. 'And do the things that will help *you* so that you can look after Robin. Isla would love to see you. She's missing her favourite doctor.'

Noa's nod was thoughtful. 'Maybe later,' he said slowly. 'I do know Robbie's safe and…it *would* be good not to feel so cut off from everything going on outside this room.'

It sounded as if there was a 'but' hanging in the air as Noa's gaze shifted to Robin and then back to Eva.

'That was a big promise you made,' he said softly. 'About his birthday.' She could see the muscles move in his throat as he swallowed. 'He trusts you,' he added, his voice almost a whisper. He didn't have to add that breaking that promise to his son would be unforgivable—the warning was hanging in the air between them.

Eva held his gaze. So this was why he'd been almost glaring at her until she'd distracted him by talking about George. Fair enough. She might not understand the undercurrents that seemed to be associated with the celebration of his son's birthday, but she certainly understood—and respected—his determination to protect his family and they both knew that it might be a big ask for Robin to be home in time for Christmas, let alone his birthday.

Her words were as quiet as his had been. 'I don't make promises I can't keep.'

Eva might not yet know exactly how she was

going to make Robin's birthday party the best ever but it had to happen.

Because she knew that trust was the foundation of the most important thing in life.

Love.

That trust wasn't going to be broken on her watch. Not for anyone, but especially not for a small motherless boy who needed as much love in his life as he could be given.

It started with just a quick visit to see George and talk to his family before he was discharged home and then to Isla to apologise for having been absent. Like everyone else, she knew that his son had been seriously unwell and nobody was blaming him for abandoning patients—they were simply delighted to see him again.

And it felt good.

So good he did it again the next day. And then he made himself available for any emergencies that were evolving on the ward when there were no other doctors available. Robin's condition improved enough for it to become easier for him to be entertained by his nurses and that meant that he didn't feel so guilty that his breaks away from his son's bedside became a little longer every day.

He was used to his dad being away for work, though, wasn't he? It had been like this for his entire life, after the blur of those first horrendous months when he could barely cope with caring for a newborn, let alone hang onto the anchor that was the job that was such an important part of who he was. It had been his mother who had encouraged him to go back to work in those dark days. What Eva had said to him the other day had reminded him of what his mother, Miriama, had said years ago, when even the thought of wanting to be away from his precious baby felt as if he was a failure as a father.

'You are his tamā, Noa—the most important person in his life—but if you don't do what makes you happy, you won't be able to make him happy.'

And they were both wise women. It wasn't simply that he needed to provide for his son—his work as a doctor had been so much of who he was from the time he'd dreamed of going to medical school. From well before he'd met Sara and for a long time before his single fatherhood had begun vying for priority. His persona as a doctor and that of a father were two halves of a whole. Keeping a balance between them might feel like a roller-coaster sometimes but it was essential for his own wellbeing. Even a limited involvement again now, especially with the children he'd known and treated for a long time, like Isla, had lifted some of the heaviness Noa hadn't been aware was stifling him. He knew he was smiling more often and his time with Robin was more like being at home after they'd been apart for work and school—where they had fun with each other and could make the most of the games and their time together.

Robin's latest MRI scan showed that his abscess was shrinking and his blood tests were reassurance that the best antibiotics were being used and no resistance to their effectiveness was developing. It was simply a matter of time now and the medical team was making the most of the intensive therapy that could be delivered while Robin was an inpatient. There were physiotherapy sessions to work on the weakness on his right side and speech therapy for the occasional disruptions noticed in his forgetting words or slurring a little. Quiet times of listening to stories or watching movies was important and so was sleep. Robin was having long naps and these were the best times for Noa to keep himself busy on the ward.

A morning that started with a call to the emergency department gave Noa the chance to thank both Ares and Ruby for their care of Robin when he'd been admitted and catch them up on his progress.

'Let's hope the outcome will be as good for this wee guy,' Ares said. 'His name's Tanush.

Three-year-old with abdo pain and distension that's going to need admission to get sorted. Initial bedside ultrasound shows a mass. CT's backed up at the moment but I thought you'd like to see him first.'

'Let's get the admission sorted. The paediatric ward is a much friendlier place to do a thorough assessment for a little one than being in an environment like Emergency. Better for the parents, too. I think I know just the right nurse to make things less scary.'

'Eva?' Ares was smiling. 'She certainly helped Robin when he came in. Tell her that if she gets bored with paediatrics we'll find a job for her here any day.'

Noa shook his head. He wouldn't be passing that message on. Besides, he was already busy thinking of differential diagnoses. It could be a bowel obstruction or abscess or some kind of tumour. And Ares was right. He wanted to do his own thorough examination and history-taking for any patient that was going to be transferred to his care and decide what other specialties like Oncology needed to be involved in the team. And he wanted Eva to be working by his side.

She was the perfect nurse for little Tanush. He stopped crying the moment he saw her beside the bed he was sitting on and reached out to touch the front of her scrub tunic—a white one today covered with colourful Christmas trees and an occasional elf.

'Kissmas tree,' Tanush declared.

'It is,' Eva agreed. Her smile was delighted. 'And who needs mistletoe when you've got a kissmas tree?'

It was the first time Noa had seen Tanush's parents smile.

'Can you find an elf,' Eva asked the toddler, 'while Dr Noa is looking at your tummy?'

His palpation was gentle but obviously still painful. He charted pain relief for Eva to administer.

'Put a patch on his hand too, please, Eva. We'll need IV access for some fluids. In the meantime, he could have a sip of water.' Noa had noticed that the little boy's crying had been without tears, which was a sign of dehydration. He glanced up at Tanush's mother. 'Has he been eating and drinking normally?'

She shook her head. 'He won't eat anything. Even his favourite cookies. And when he had some orange juice it made him sick.'

Eva held Tanush when Noa inserted the IV line and took blood samples. She went with him to his CT scan and Noa reviewed the results later in consultation with the oncology team. The pain relief had made their patient far more comfortable and IV fluids were helping to reverse the effects of dehydration, but Noa had to talk to Tanush's family about the next steps of treatment and he knew it was going to be an intense and upsetting discussion. Surgery was scheduled first thing tomorrow morning to take a biopsy of the abdominal mass the scan had revealed in detail and some warning needed to be given that the information the invasive test would provide could be a life-changing diagnosis that would affect the whole family.

He'd ask Eva to talk to them too, when she had some time. He knew that doctors could be more intimidating than nurses and people were reluctant to ask too many questions. He knew that Tanush's family would have a lot more questions when they'd had time to process the potentially devastating diagnosis that could come from tomorrow's biopsy. He also now knew, from personal experience, just how empathetic and kind Eva was.

It was no surprise to find her in Robin's room, but Noa was surprised to find his son looking less than happy.

'Bella's going to come and look after you,' Eva was telling him. 'I've promised Isla I'll help with her physio this afternoon.'

'But I want you to look after *me*...' Robin's bottom lip was wobbling but and Noa could see that Eva hated to be letting him down so he thought fast.

'How 'bout I get a wheelchair?' he asked. 'I think you'd be okay to be out of bed for a bit and I bet you'd like to see the Christmas tree that's downstairs by the front doors of the hospital. I think it might be the biggest Christmas tree in the whole world.'

'What a great idea.' If Eva's glance wasn't enough to thank him for making it easier for her to do what she had to do and spend time with other patients, her smile certainly was.

Even better, Robin was smiling as well.

Noa tucked him into a wheelchair, pushing him with one hand because he needed the other one to hang onto the IV pole. They took the lift down to the ground floor and the change of scene and the excitement of all the decorations to be spotted on their journey was making Robin happier than he'd seen him since he'd been admitted to hospital. There was a Christmas sleigh frieze on a wall, being pulled by a whole herd of reindeer, big paper bells in bright colours hanging from the entrance to the shops in the foyer, like the pharmacy and gift shop, and the main reception desk was a work of art in tinsel.

What captured attention instantly, however, was the magnificent Christmas tree that dominated the whole height of this bright, airy space.

Robin gazed up in total awe as Noa wheeled him closer, his mouth agape for some time.

'What can you see?' he asked.

'Pretty lights,' Robin said. 'And…red apples and little boxes like presents and…' His voice was a sigh of wonder. 'Look at the star on top, Daddy. Can we put a star on our tree, too?'

'Of course we can.' Not that Noa had given the slightest thought to any decorations at home yet. There was plenty of time. Robin's grandparents weren't arriving until the day before Christmas Eve and that…well, it was weeks away. He didn't need to think about it yet.

'We won't get one quite this big, though,' he said.

Robin giggled. 'That would be silly,' he said. 'It wouldn't fit in our house.'

'No. And do you know, the person who put the star on that tree fell off the ladder and he broke his leg and had to have an operation.'

'Like me,' Robin breathed. 'Is he getting better now?'

'I think so.' Noa ruffled his son's hair. 'Just like you. Shall we go back upstairs now? You can see the tree that Eva decorated that's in our ward.'

Robin craned his neck to get a last look at the big tree. 'I love Christmas trees,' he said happily.

Noa wanted to agree. He wanted to say that he loved Christmas trees too, but he couldn't.

Because it wasn't true.

He dreaded this time of year. He had to grit his teeth at every single reminder of Christmas because it was also a reminder of the worst time of his life, when his world had gone in an instant from being as perfect as it got—with his dream job, his beloved wife and their first baby about to arrive—to a nightmare he'd never contemplated having to live through.

Last year had been the hardest. He couldn't even remember that first Christmas, within days of Robin's birth. A year later, he'd still been no more than a baby and Noa had used the holiday season to visit his parents in New Zealand where the summer weather made it feel as if it wasn't really Christmas at all. As a two-year-old, Robin still hadn't been aware that a few token decorations and a special present were less than other children had. As a three-year-old, however, the magic of the season was making an impression and it had been time to step up and make it special. This year, it was going to be their first real family Christmas because Noa had invited his parents to come and stay.

They had, of course, offered to travel as soon as they'd heard of Robin's illness but Noa had persuaded them to wait. Their travel plans were all in place, there was a good chance Robin would be discharged by then and it would be much better for them all to be together at home for the visit rather than trapped within the walls of a hospital.

He would make a new start, Noa decided, as they waited for the lift to come back to the ground floor. He wasn't going to go into the attic and get the decorations that Sara had put up in the house—the ones that he'd torn down and stuffed into boxes and then thrown into the attic to get rid of them so that he didn't have to come home to a totally inappropriately jolly atmosphere in those first dreadful days.

No. He'd order brand-new Christmas decorations online.

He'd turn the house into a Christmas grotto to welcome both his parents and Robin's return home.

And it didn't matter that he had no idea where to start because he knew someone who was an expert in Christmas decorations and he could be quite sure she'd be only too happy to help him.

Robin was yawning. 'I love Christmas trees,' he said again as the lift doors closed in front of him. Then he looked up at his father and smiled. 'I love Eva, too.'

Noa blinked. Was it some weird kind of telepathy or had they both been thinking about Eva

Mason, for different reasons, at exactly the same time? But it wasn't that strange, was it? She was a big part of their lives right now and she was helping him care for the most important person in the world to him.

Noa's heart was melting as he smiled down at Robin.

Oh, man...that look in those big, dark eyes—the love shining out of them—took his breath away and squeezed his heart with the sudden surge of love for his son, and what rushed in afterwards was such a wave of relief that Robin was recovering from something that could have taken him away for ever that Noa could feel tears prickling at the back of his eyes.

He leaned down so that his mouth was right beside Robin's little shell of an ear.

'And I love *you*, monkey,' he said, his voice catching. 'All the way to the moon and back.'

The excitement of his first adventure away from his room had been almost too much for Robin. He was ready for a sleep by the time Noa had him back in his bed and Eva had taken and recorded vital sign measurements like his temperature, heart and respiration rates and his pulse oximeter reading. All it took for him to drift into a deep, restful sleep was reading the first few pages of a favourite book to him, but it looked as if Noa was having trouble keeping his own eyes open as he did so.

'When did you last have a decent sleep?' she asked him quietly.

Noa shrugged. 'I get enough.'

'In that chair? When you're going to wake up with every sound or movement that Robin makes?' Eva frowned. 'Have you even used the on-call room they've put aside for you and actually slept in a bed?'

Noa rubbed his forehead with his fingers but he was shaking his head slowly at the same time.

'I don't like to,' he said. 'Especially during night shift hours. I remember what it was like to be on call as a junior doc and being so exhausted that getting my head down just for an hour or two was a lifesaver.'

'There's more than one on-call room,' Eva reminded him. 'And it's not night shift yet. Robin's going to sleep for an hour or more now. Why don't you go and lie down? Even if you don't sleep, it would still be a better rest than being in here. Bella can come and stay with Robin while I'm next door with Isla's physio session and one of us will come and get you as soon as he wakes up.'

It looked as if Noa was too weary to summon any kind of argument. 'Promise?'

'Yes.' Eva swallowed hard as she held his gaze.

'Okay, then… Sounds good.' She could see the effort it took for Noa to push himself to his feet but he was moving. He was going to go to the on-call room and try and get an hour or two's sleep—like he used to do as an overworked junior doctor.

She didn't need him to say anything to remind her that she'd told him she didn't make promises she couldn't keep.

This had just become an unspoken test.

CHAPTER FIVE

BELLA CAME TO watch Robin while Eva went back to Isla's room.

The slow response of Isla's lung function to the antibiotics that were fighting the chest infection had led to a decision to increase the respiratory physiotherapy she was receiving in both frequency and variety. Eva had been with her for her PEP session while Robin had been away admiring the Christmas tree, which involved using a device that made it easy to breathe in but harder to breathe out, but the effort had been too much for it to have the desired effect. They were going to try something different now, which was an oscillating vest that Isla could wear. Hopefully, it would loosen the infected mucus in her lungs and move it high enough for it to be easier for her to get rid of it by coughing.

Eva's heart went out to the brave twelve-year-old as she helped fasten a rather bulky vest around a chest where every rib was visible. She helped make her comfortable against her pillows as the physio hooked up the tubes that connected the vest to the impulse generator and adjusted the settings. Isla used her inhaler, with its spacing device, to get medication into her lungs to help the process and then the machine was turned on and the vibrations began.

'Does it hurt?' Kay was beside the bed.

'N-n-no-o—'

The vibration in Isla's voice made them all smile and the session suddenly became…well… not quite fun, but definitely tolerable.

Every five minutes, the machine was turned off and Isla was encouraged to do her huffing.

'Breathe in through your nose,' the physio said. 'Slowly… Hold your breath for three seconds…one, two, three… Now, use the muscles in your tummy and push that air out. Make your mouth a big O and keep pushing…'

'Good girl.' Eva was holding her hand. 'You're doing a great job.'

Isla needed to do three of these low-level huffs and then three high level huffs where she added a sniff to the inhalation to get even more air into her lungs and the exhalation was quick and forceful enough to make it a cough.

After a short rest, the steps were repeated. By the third set of high-level huffs, enough mucus had been expelled to make a real difference when the usual measure of lung function was done.

'That's the best peak flow reading you've had since you were admitted,' Eva told her. 'Way to go, Isla.'

Kay gave her daughter a hug. 'I'm so proud of you, darling. That was hard work, wasn't it?'

Isla simply nodded.

Eva gave her a sip of her drink. 'Have a rest,' she said. She caught Kay's gaze. 'I'll tell the charge nurse at handover to put her dinner aside if she's asleep when the trolley arrives. You can heat it up in the microwave later.'

It had taken nearly an hour with the stops for the breathing exercises and the medication before and after the treatment for Isla but Robin was still asleep when Eva returned. She could only hope Noa was as well, because he wasn't in the room.

'I'll stay until he wakes up,' Eva told Bella. 'If I'm late for handover, Nicole's got my notes.'

Daylight faded so fast at this time of the year. It was only late afternoon but it looked like night-time outside and Eva stood for a long moment, enjoying the lights along the river and in the city. She hadn't been in to admire all the decorations in town yet but she knew she'd be in for a treat when she did. The streets of York, like the famous Shambles with its cobbles and quirky buildings and Fossgate and Grape Lane and many others were already gorgeous, but the lights and pretty decorations for Christmas took everything to another level completely. The only reason Eva hadn't gone already was that she didn't want to go alone. She was waiting for one of her friends, like Ruby or Bella, to be available or for when her sister would take the children in for one of the light shows or to visit the Christmas market on Parliament Street and ride the vintage carousel in King's Square.

As if he knew she was thinking about things that children would love, Robin stirred and opened his eyes.

'Where's Daddy?'

'He's been having a sleep, just like you, sweetheart. Do you want me to go and find him?'

'Yes…'

'Will you be okay by yourself for a minute?'

'Yes.' Robin's nod was solemn. 'I'm going to be *four*.'

'Of course you are.' Eva smiled. 'And look, here's the bell. I'll put it on your bed and if you need someone before I get back, you push it and someone like Bella will come and look after you.'

It felt like night-time in the ward too. Eva tapped lightly on the door of the on-call room but there was no response. She tapped again and then opened the door quietly.

'Noa?'

There was still no response and Eva's heart skipped a beat. Was Noa even in here? She stepped in and waited for her eyes to adjust to the darkness. Yes, she could see the shape of him on the bed and hear the slow, steady breathing of deep sleep.

She didn't want to wake him.

But she *had* to keep her promise.

She touched his arm lightly. 'Noa?'

He woke up with a start and she had to step back as he not only sat up but instantly swung his legs over the side of the bed and stood up.

'Sorry,' Eva said. 'I didn't mean to give you a fright.'

Or maybe she was the one getting the fright because she had this big man so near her in such a confined space. Towering over her, in fact.

No wonder her heart was racing so fast she could feel the pulse of her blood in her finger-tips and toes.

He was so close she could feel the heat of his body and smell an aroma she recognised that was definitely not any kind of shampoo or soap. It was pure Noa.

Smoky. Musky.

And drop-dead *sexy*…

Eva knew her eyes were too wide and her gasp of breath was audible but she couldn't look away.

Because Noa was staring back at her and he looked…

He looked as though he was aware of what was rushing through her mind—and her body.

This…*awareness*…that hung there like a hum of sound around them.

Or—oh, *help*…was it desire?

Whatever.

It couldn't happen.

Even if it looked as if Noa was just as aware of it as she was.

'Sorry,' Eva said again, and it felt as if she was apologising for having inappropriate thoughts about someone who had—and never would—think of her as anything other than a colleague. 'I did knock but you didn't hear me.'

'Is Robin awake?'

'Yes.' Eva stepped back again. 'He asked where you were and said he'd like me to come and get you.'

Noa was already moving. 'Thanks.'

Eva waited a beat and then followed him out of the room. The lights felt bright enough out here to obliterate any shadows of what had just happened and there was no lingering scent of the man who'd been asleep in that bed.

Thank goodness for that.

For once, Eva couldn't wait for handover and the opportunity to escape.

She left the Royal at the end of her shift with the comfort of knowing that she had a whole day off tomorrow. She intended to finish her Christmas shopping and spend some time with her family. Hopefully, by the time she was back to work, Noa would have pushed that disturbing little encounter out of his mind.

Which was exactly what she intended to do herself.

'Is Eva going to be here today?'

'I think so. As far as I know, yesterday was her only day off for this week.'

'I missed her.' Robin's tone was plaintive. 'Why did she have a day off?'

'Everybody needs a day off sometimes. Especially people that work as hard as Eva does. She can't be here all the time. She's got things to do at home, too.'

'Like what?'

Noa blinked. What *did* Eva do with her time away from the Royal?

'I don't know,' he admitted. 'But I'm sure she's got lots of friends. And a family of her own.'

'Has she got a little boy? Like me?'

'Um… I don't think so.'

Noa knew that Eva wasn't married, but that didn't preclude having children, did it? A memory was trying to surface from the blur of those

first few horrific hours when Robin had been
admitted, nearly two weeks ago now. The way
she'd stayed with him as he waited while his
son's future was so uncertain. Her quiet presence
that hadn't suggested she had anywhere else in
the world that she wanted to be right then. And
what about how often she'd stayed with Robin
out of her work hours? Surely she wouldn't have
made herself so available if she had a partner or
children waiting for her at home?

No. He could be sure that the people closest
to Eva Mason would be as important to her as
Robin was to himself. He wouldn't let anyone
else steal any of the time that never felt quite
enough anyway to be the person he wanted to
be for his son. Despite how big he knew Eva's
heart was, he could be sure that her priorities
would be just as sacrosanct.

Which probably also meant she didn't have
a partner.

If she did, that odd moment in the on-call
room would be even more awkward. Noa wasn't
at all sure what had happened exactly. He just
knew that it was proving almost impossible to
forget and it was disturbing him, as if he'd somehow been unfaithful to Sara's memory by noticing another woman.

He'd never noticed another woman since he'd

lost Sara. Not in a sexual way, that was for sure. He simply wasn't interested.

But the feeling was still trying to ambush him. Fighting it off made it an effort to focus on what he was doing, which was to let Robin try on his soft-shell helmet that he would need to wear for his first physiotherapy session in the gym this afternoon.

He settled the padded sections amongst the waves of Robin's hair, measured the chin straps and then adjusted the length before clicking the buckle into place.

'Fantastic,' he pronounced. 'You look like you're ready to jump onto your motorbike and ride off into the sunset to fight dragons. And pink was the best colour to choose.'

But Robin wasn't listening. He was watching the door. Willing his day shift nurse to arrive?

'I like it better when Eva's looking after me.'

'I know, monkey.' Was Robin getting too attached to Eva? Enough that it would make things harder when he was back home and only had his dad and the intermittent help he had from babysitters? At least he'd have the distraction of having his grandparents around for a while to bridge the gap.

'We had fun yesterday, though, didn't we?' he asked. 'You got to make those awesome Christmas cards with Jules.'

The occupational therapist had brought a lot of craft materials like cardboard and glitter, crayons and stickers. She'd encouraged Robin to use his right hand as much as possible, but Noa could see that the weakness was still noticeable and his writing, which had been astonishingly good for his age, was almost illegible.

In effect, an infection like an abscess could cause as much damage as a traumatic injury and only time would tell if it was permanent. With the same weakness in his right leg, he would also need therapy to walk again and the start of that was on today's agenda in the physiotherapy department.

'Shall we take your helmet off again for now? You don't need to wear it while you're having your breakfast.'

'No. I want Eva to see it.'

Which she did, only moments later, as she came into the room with the breakfast tray.

'Morning, sweetheart.' She didn't meet Noa's gaze as she put the tray on the table and swivelled it so it was over the bed, but he could feel that something was different.

'Do you like my hat?'

'I love it.'

Yes. The smile might be just as wide as always but it wasn't reaching Eva's eyes. Something was wrong and Noa had a horrible feeling it might have something to do with that moment in the on-call room.

'Let's see what you've got for breakfast. Are you hungry?'

'Yes.'

'That's good. Because I just heard that you're going to the gym this morning so you're going to need lots of energy. Ooh, look...' Eva lifted a cloche. 'You've got an egg and some toast soldiers to dip into it. Yum... I'm guessing you're going to eat up every bit of it.'

Her encouragement was the same as always too, but her enthusiasm felt dulled this morning. Noa helped Robin dip the end of the thin slice of toast into his egg yolk with his right hand. He knew she was aware of his gaze and eventually she looked up to meet it. He tried to erase the frown he could feel on his brow by raising his eyebrows. And letting his lips curve into the hint of a smile.

It was a silent query to ask if she was okay. And something softened in her eyes for a fraction of time, as if she appreciated his concern, but then she simply nodded, giving him a silent response that she was fine.

It was obvious that she wasn't. But it wasn't any of his business. Or was it? If this had anything to do with him, he needed to find a way to reassure her that whatever odd vibe had been there between them in the on-call room, it meant nothing. If he'd been giving off signals that had been misinterpreted, it was only because he'd been under so much stress, exacerbated by lack of sleep.

Now wasn't the time, however.

Noa excused himself as soon as Robin had finished his breakfast and Eva was getting ready to take the daily blood sample. He walked towards the door where she was collecting the supplies she needed from the bench beside the basin.

'I'll head off for a bit. I'm hoping to get to the gym and see what Robbie's getting up to this afternoon and I've got quite a lot on, so I might just go and get started with my ward round early. I'm wondering what sort of night Tanush and his family had.'

'I heard about him at handover.' Eva was sticking Robin's ID labels to the test tubes. 'How hard would it be to get a diagnosis like that right before Christmas?'

'It's early stage. But it is high-risk so he'll need chemo after surgery. He's getting a central line inserted this morning and the major surgery is scheduled for tomorrow.'

Tanush's parents, grandparents and an auntie or two were all with the little boy and Noa's heart went out to them all.

He gave as much reassurance as he could by focusing on the fact that they'd caught this cancer at an early stage and that new and better treatment for neuroblastomas, in both the surgical and drug treatment, meant that more and more children were not only surviving but being cured. He talked them through the procedure of inserting the central line which would provide a port that would make administration of IV drugs and fluids painless and also talked about the surgery planned to remove the tumour tomorrow. He arranged to get someone from Paediatric Oncology to come and go over the chemotherapy regime again, but that could wait a few days.

There was only so much the family could take in and remember and with the grandparents needing translation it was a slow process. But Noa knew what it was like to be on the parents' side of this equation now and it made him take as much time as was needed to patiently repeat things and answer any questions.

He did get to the physiotherapy department in time to see Robin looking very wobbly, on his feet for the first time since his admission. He was just standing and not walking but his face lit up when he saw his father.

'Daddy... I can go for a swim tomorrow.'

'We've got a lovely hot pool,' the physio added.

'It's a great way of easing back into weightbearing with movement.'

'Wow…that's exciting. I'll have to get home later today and find your swimming trunks.'

He could have yet another hunt for that elusive Sheepy toy too, although Robin seemed quite happy to be sleeping with his new favourite—the Santa-elf that Eva had given him.

He had another gift from the physio to take back to the ward, which was a squishy stress ball in the shape of a Santa.

'Squeeze him every time you remember. Especially with your right hand. Do you remember which hand is the right one?'

Robin shook his head but his smile charmed the physio into grinning back at him. 'Just as well I've got my special stamp, then.' She pressed it onto the back of Robin's right hand.

'It's a Christmas tree,' he said delightedly. 'We're going to get a Christmas tree at home that's as big as the one that man fell off.'

'Really? You must have a very big house.' She was still smiling as she looked up at Noa. 'It will be really helpful if you can bring Robin's trunks and maybe a dressing gown to keep him warm after his swim. You're welcome to come in the pool with him if you'd like to.'

It was past time for the shift changeover and already getting dark outside when Robin was finally back in his bed but he wasn't upset that he'd missed saying goodnight to Eva. It was reassuring that he seemed more than happy to curl up with a story and then a sleep with Bella looking after him. Maybe he wasn't getting too attached to Eva after all.

'You have to go home, Daddy,' he told Noa. 'You have to find my swimming trunks. The ones with the fish on them.'

'Okay, monkey. I'll be back later.'

Noa hadn't expected to see Eva as he walked through the foyer a short time later. She was in her civvies, with jeans tucked into boots visible under a puffy anorak with a faux-fur trim on the hood. She had a red woollen hat in her hand that had silver stars on it and a bag over her shoulder but she was standing still, admiring the huge Christmas tree.

'Robbie wants one just like this at home,' he said, by way of a greeting.

Eva didn't say anything. She was blinking hard, Noa noticed and…oh, no…was she catching a tear that had escaped to roll down the side of her nose?

He wasn't going to ask whether she was okay and give her the chance to brush him off. Instead, he pretended he hadn't seen that she was crying.

'Are you rushing home for anything?' he asked.

Eva shook her head. 'Not really.'

'Good.' Noa gave her his best smile. 'I need some fresh air and I'd love some company. Come with me?'

He could see the reflection of the coloured lighting twinkling on the tree in her eyes—probably because they were still brimming with some leftover tears. The level of sadness they represented was both unexpected and heartbreaking.

And he remembered what she'd said about providing him with all those coffees and sandwiches. That she was paying it forward because you never knew when you might need a bit of kindness yourself.

She needed it now. And the urge to be the one to provide it was astonishingly strong.

'Please?' he added very softly.

It was that smile that had done it.

Or perhaps it had been the way he'd looked at her. As though he could see into her soul and he knew exactly how horrible her day had been. The last two days, in fact, because the news she'd received yesterday had completely wrecked her day off. Immersing herself in the joy of Christmas shopping would have only made her feel worse and spending time with her niece and nephew was the last thing she felt up to doing, so she'd shut herself away from the world, which had only thrown her deeper into the hole.

At least Eva had made herself go to work today. She'd even managed to put a bright smile on her face and behave as if nothing had happened.

Noa had seen through that pretty much the moment she'd walked into Robin's room, hadn't he?

Maybe it was the look that had really done it—the way he'd raised his eyebrows and silently asked her if she was okay. Offering to become involved in whatever had happened in her personal life, if she wanted him to be. She'd brushed him off then but when he'd found her crying in front of the big Christmas tree Eva hadn't been able to summon the strength to pretend that everything was all right.

And being alone was the last thing she wanted to be right now.

So here she was, walking along the riverbank with Noa Jones, past the Memorial Gardens towards the city centre. They walked in a companionable silence and crossed the river on Lendal Bridge, stopping by tacit consent beneath the ornate antique streetlamps to admire the canal boats and other vessels moored in front of the Museum Gardens and lit up to celebrate the season as brightly as any Christmas tree.

One long boat had frosted lights that looked like icicles dripping from the edges of the deck all the way from the bow to the stern. Another had a large inflatable reindeer tied to a mast and one had Santa in a sleigh on top of the cabin. The sound of Christmas carols drifted up from a boat tethered close to the bridge. The haunting notes of 'O Holy Night' resonated deeply with how she was feeling at the moment so it wasn't surprising that it moved her almost to tears again.

Neither was it surprising that Noa somehow noticed, even though it was dark and they were both leaning on the parapet and looking at the river. The music was quiet enough to be easy to speak over.

'What is it, Eva? I hope it's not something *I've* done that's upset you.'

Oh, God…was Noa thinking that her state of mind was connected to that moment in the on-call room? Had he seen how she was feeling and thought she was now nursing a broken heart due to rejection?

'*No*,' she said swiftly and possibly a little too vehemently. 'It's… I got some news yesterday that upset me, that's all.'

There. She hadn't even been at work yesterday so Noa could be reassured that it had nothing to do with him. He could stop being so concerned.

Or maybe not.

'I've never seen you like this,' he said softly. 'Talk to me, Eva...'

'It's ancient history, really.' She tried to make it sound unimportant. 'It should have been over years ago when my marriage ended.'

'The things that happened in our past make us who we are today,' Noa said. 'They might end but the loss stays with us for ever and there's no timeline for grief. It's nothing to be ashamed of if it still sneaks up on you and gives you a punch in the gut.'

Eva said nothing as she absorbed the wisdom. She could feel Noa's gaze resting on her face.

'Was he a bit stupid—your ex-husband?'

She blinked. 'No. He's a consultant anaesthetist now. Head of department, in fact. Why would you say that?'

'He's not with you any longer, is he?'

Eva's breath came out in a short huff of laughter. It made a little cloud in the cold evening air.

'We got married too young,' she found herself saying—almost as if this was no more than a casual conversation between close friends. How could it possibly feel this comfortable, talking about something this personal to Noa?

Something this private?

Was it because she'd been allowed close

enough to share something that had been so very private for him? That fear of losing his only child.

'We were only in our early twenties,' she added. 'Turned out the timing was wrong. I was ready to start a family. Aaron said he was too but, looking back, it was obvious he was relieved when I couldn't get pregnant.'

'Did they find a cause?'

'No. We jumped through various hoops for years but finally got accepted for IVF treatment. That's what broke us up.'

Noa was silent for a moment. 'I've heard that the intensity of the treatment can put an unbearable pressure on relationships. Especially if it fails.'

'Didn't get a chance to fail,' Eva said dryly. 'Our marriage ended when Aaron told me there was something I should know before we went to our first appointment and took the process any further.'

'Which was?'

'That he'd been having an affair with some administrative assistant at the hospital we both worked at. Janine, her name was. It had been going on for over a year by then. That's when I gave up. On being married to him or being able to have a baby.'

'He didn't deserve you,' Noa growled.

The protective note in his voice was comforting.

'I don't know about that,' Eva murmured.

'I do,' Noa said decisively. 'You're the best paediatric nurse I've ever worked with and it's not just Robbie who adores you. In my experience, kids are good judges of who the best people in this world are.' He cleared his throat, as if he felt he'd said too much. 'How long ago did you escape your marriage?'

Escape? He made it sound as if it had been a proactive choice on her part. And that she hadn't actually been such a failure.

'Long enough that I should be over it,' Eva responded. 'And I am. It's just that…well…yesterday I heard that he and Janine have just had their first baby and…' Her voice trailed off.

'It hurts,' Noa finished for her. 'I get that.'

They stood in silence for a minute after that. The more cheerful notes of 'Jingle Bells' were in the background now and Noa straightened, rubbing his hands together as if he was cold. Or wanted to move on?

'I still owe you for all those coffees, not to mention the sandwiches you gave me when I needed them the most. Let's go somewhere so I can return the favour.'

'Like where?'

'Let's follow our noses. Or where everybody else seems to be heading. Have you got time?'

'Yes. But have you? Don't you want to get back to Robin?'

'It's good for both of us to get a break. He'll still be sound asleep after all the excitement of the outing to Physio today. And he's got Bella when he wakes up. He loves her almost as much as you.' Noa's smile was brief. 'Come on…'

CHAPTER SIX

IT TURNED OUT that the flow of pedestrians going
past them were all heading for the Christmas
markets in St Samson's Square and The Shambles. They mingled with the crowd in the vil-
lage of wooden alpine chalets where there was
a huge array of Christmas goodies for sale. So
many crafts and potential gifts like jewellery,
clothing and children's toys. There were candles and soap and dried flowers and Christmas
wreaths, seasonal jumpers, chocolate and nou-
gat and Christmas trees, lights and decorations.
There was more than one chalet offering hot food
and drinks like mulled wine and hot chocolate.

'Can I get you a hot chocolate instead of a coffee?' Noa asked.

'I'd love one. Thank you... I'm going to look
around while you're in the queue if you don't
mind. I've still got some Christmas gifts I need
to find.'

'Good idea. I'll come and find you.'

Eva knew her twelve-year-old niece, Hay-

ley, would love some Christmas earrings so she
headed for the jewellery chalet, but she got distracted on the way by an awning that had Christmas decorations dangling from hooks. Amongst
them, she spotted a dear little robin with a bright
red bib, little feet attached to a twig and its beak
open as if it was singing. Without hesitation,
Eva took it off its hook and paid for it, getting it
wrapped up in tissue paper to put in her shoulder bag.

It would be a Christmas gift for Robin Jones
from Nurse Eva. Maybe he would keep it and remember his time in hospital with her for years
to come. She moved swiftly on and bought some
little Christmas pudding earrings for both Hayley and herself and it was while they were being
wrapped that Noa came up to her, holding two
paper cups.

The chocolate was hot and thick and had
melted marshmallow on the top and it was delicious. They kept walking as they sipped, still
following the flow of people out enjoying the
markets. A few minutes later, they found themselves in King's Square where the gorgeous vintage carousel was glowing under lights strung
beneath its colourful canopy and the traditional,
slightly tinny music was getting louder with
every step closer they took.

'I love this carousel,' Eva said. 'I fell in love

with these horses when I was Robin's age. Has he had a ride on it yet?'

'No.' Noa was frowning as he watched the riders of the prancing wooden horses with their flowing manes and tails, as they hung onto the twisted poles and got swept around and up and down. 'He's old enough to hang on safely now but it's not something I'm going to let him do too soon. He might need to be on his anti-seizure medication for quite a long time.'

'Oh... I didn't think of that.' Eva bit her lip. She had been watching the horses as well, but when she shifted her gaze to Noa, about to say that she was sorry he was going to miss the fun this year, she found him turning to look at her at exactly the same moment. They stared at each other and it felt as if the idea was as mutual as meeting each other's gaze. Or had Eva somehow telepathically planted the idea in Noa's head? Big, fierce men weren't known for wanting to do frivolous things like ride a merry-go-round, were they?

But Noa lifted an eyebrow. 'Shall we?'

Eva grinned. 'I think it would be rude not to, don't you?'

It was Noa who bought the tickets. They didn't have to wait long for the carousel to come to a halt and the riders to dismount. They climbed up and Eva chose a caramel-coloured horse with a green saddle and Noa took the one beside her which was white with a red saddle. Moments later they were off and there was something wonderfully nostalgic and carefree about doing something she hadn't done since she was a child. The misery of the last couple of days was evaporating into the chill of the evening air and Eva could tell herself—and, more importantly, believe it—that she had so much to be grateful for in her life. That she was happier than she'd been in a very long time.

Noa glanced at his watch as their ride finished. 'I might have to head back,' he said apologetically.

'Of course.'

'Which way are you going?'

'Back to the Royal. My car's in the staff car park.'

'That's good. I want to get back, but I wasn't going to leave you to walk home alone.'

There was that protective streak again. Eva liked it. A lot.

'Do you mind if we take a slight detour? I promised that I'd go home and find Robbie's swimming trunks. The physio is going to get him into the pool tomorrow and he's thrilled by the idea.'

'I don't mind at all,' Eva assured him. She was, in fact, intrigued by the thought that she was going to see where this mysterious colleague of hers lived and what his home might be like.

Because she liked *him*, she realised.

A lot.

It was only a ten-minute walk from the carousel to Noa's street, which was lined on both sides with charming brick houses that dated back to the mid-nineteenth century and were still protected by their original wrought-iron fences.

He unlocked the front door and switched lights on in the hallway. The staircase curved up on one side at the end.

'The lounge is just through there.' Noa pointed at a doorway. 'Make yourself at home. It shouldn't take me more than a few minutes to collect everything that Robbie needs for swimming, grab a few things for myself and to have another look for that damn Sheepy toy. I can't believe that something so important to him has been lost.'

'Have you asked him if he knows where it is?'

'No. I didn't want him to start missing it. Or realise that it's been lost.'

'Is it possible he took it to school with him?'

'I never thought of that.' Noa paused at the bottom of the stairs. 'But it's a good thought. I'll give them a ring tomorrow.'

Eva had turned the light on in the lounge as

Noa began climbing the stairs. 'Oh, my…' he heard her call. 'What a gorgeous room. I *love* the fireplace. And that ceiling rose.'

These days, Noa barely noticed the period features that both he and Sara had fallen in love with when they were property-hunting. It was being able to walk to the Royal via the Museum Gardens that had been the only reason he'd chosen to stay somewhere that had held such painful memories for such a long time. Oh…and the fact that there were enough bedrooms to make it easy for his parents to stay or when he needed an overnight babysitter.

And…he flicked on the light in Robin's bedroom…there was *this*. The room that let a little boy know just how much his mother had loved him even before he'd been born. There was so much love in every detail, but she'd been especially proud of the frieze of painted robins she'd found to go around the walls.

'I'm going to tell him how special robins are— that they're a symbol of good luck and happiness. Did you know that in Celtic mythology they're seen as messengers, connecting people with loved ones who have died?'

Noa's mother, Miriama, had discovered that somewhere. She was the one who'd put the white wooden heart over the head of Robin's bed. There was a cute robin—as round as a golf ball, painted on one side of that heart, along with the words *'Robins appear when loved ones are near'*.

'That'll be your mummy,' Miriama had told Robin. *'Telling you how much she loves you and that she wants you to be as happy as you can possibly be.'*

He was going to be happy when he got to go swimming tomorrow. Noa was smiling as opened a drawer and found the swimming trunks with the fish on them. He found the beach towel that featured undersea creatures from one of Robin's favourite movies and grabbed a fuzzy dressing gown and socks that would keep him warm after his swim. He had another quick look for Sheepy, but maybe Eva was right and the toy had been secretly taken to school. It took another minute or two to find fresh clothes for himself to take back and then he went back downstairs.

Eva wasn't in the first lounge with the bay window and big fireplace, or the second one with the piano and toy corner that led to both the kitchen and the conservatory which was also their dining room. That was where he found Eva, peering out through the glass panes of the French windows into the long, narrow garden, dimly illuminated by streetlights.

'Your house is just beautiful,' she told him.

'Robin must love this garden.' She bit her lip. 'Looks like there's enough room for a dog.'

Noa made a groaning sound. 'Don't you start. I've got quite enough on my plate without trying to juggle another family member. But yeah…it's a nice garden and it backs onto another street so I've got dual access and off-street parking— behind that little summer house.'

'I envy you being able to walk to work.' Eva was moving back towards him. 'Can you go through the Museum Gardens? It's one of my favourite places.'

'Robin's, too.' Noa turned to lead her through the living area towards the front hall. 'He's in love with St Mary's Abbey.'

Eva paused to glance over her shoulder as she reached the door he was holding open for her. Was she looking at all the photographs of Sara he had on top of the piano? Her eyebrows were raised as she glanced at him and it was then he realised that this was the first time he'd brought a woman into this house since Sara had died. It could well turn out to have been a huge mistake if she wanted to push him back into the past by asking personal questions.

But his past was apparently not what Eva was thinking about.

'You haven't had time to put your Christmas

decorations up,' she said. 'Or do you usually wait until after Robin's birthday to do that?'

'Ah...' Good grief... Robin's birthday was only a couple of days away and while he had some gifts he knew were on the longed-for list that he'd purchased some time ago and hidden away for both the birthday and Christmas, he hadn't organised any kind of party yet. His inspiration to turn this house into a Christmas grotto on top of birthday preparations and everything else that needed to be done before his parents arrived to stay, like getting the spare room ready and doing a massive grocery shop, suddenly seemed overwhelming.

A bit like all those intentions he'd ever had to be the best father a boy could have and then to find himself simply lurching from one day to the next, barely coping.

Eva was looking up at him curiously in the beat of silence.

'I was going to talk to you about that,' he admitted. 'I want to buy new decorations for the house this year. I'm thinking of doing it online and having them delivered, but I might need a bit of help choosing them.'

That glow that had been missing from Eva's face today had already returned—probably during that ride on the carousel. But it had just gone up a notch or two and she looked genuinely joyous, her eyes shining and her lips curving into the happiest smile ever.

'I can help.' Her words were an excited whisper. 'I *love* Christmas.'

Noa was smiling back at her, watching as she caught her bottom lip between her teeth. As if he didn't know that already.

And then it happened.

He was caught.

He couldn't look away from Eva's mouth. He didn't dare raise his gaze to her eyes because he might see what he'd thought he'd seen in the on-call room the other day—that she might be seeing him as something other than a colleague or the parent of one of her patients.

That she might have been aware of what he'd been thinking. Or rather, feeling. That *attraction*.

The desire to touch her. To hold Eva in his arms.

To *kiss* her…

It was impossible not to meet her gaze now. And he was right.

Eva *wanted* him to kiss her.

For a nanosecond too long, they both held that gaze.

They both knew.

They both acknowledged the attraction.

They both knew it couldn't be allowed to happen. He didn't need to remember all the photographs of Sara in the next room to be reminded of why it couldn't be allowed to happen. He only needed to remember that it was almost Christmas. Almost Robin's birthday.

Almost the anniversary of losing Sara.

This moment had to be broken.

Noa reached past Eva to turn off the lights.

Oh...

She'd prattled too much on that final walk from Noa's house to the Royal, hadn't she? She'd barely given Noa a chance to say anything as she offered suggestions for the kind of Christmas decorations that would look so lovely in his house.

'You're so lucky to have a real fireplace. You can have red candles scented with frankincense and cinnamon on the mantelpiece and a fir tree garland, maybe with red velvet bows, and then hang a big stocking for Robin.'

Noa had just grunted.

'Some lights outside would be gorgeous, too. Like the ones your neighbours have put up. And a real Christmas tree inside so you can get that gorgeous smell right through the house. You can get them in pots now, so it could go outside onto

the patio during the year and be ready for next Christmas.'

The walk only took ten minutes but she'd found time to talk about Robin's birthday as well.

'We need balloons. And party hats and a cake. I'm working on a special surprise.'

'Which is?'

'I won't tell you yet, in case I can't make it happen.'

It sounded as if Noa might have sighed at that point. Maybe he was simply relieved that they'd reached the parking area for the Royal and Eva would be getting into her car any second and they wouldn't have to find anything else to talk about to fill any silence.

So they wouldn't have to talk about what had just happened.

Or, rather, hadn't happened.

That kiss that had been there, hanging in the air, within such easy reach.

For just an instant, she knew they'd both wanted to catch it. She knew she hadn't been mistaken the other day in the on-call room. Noa could feel it too. That hum.

That—almost—irresistible attraction that, somehow, Noa had managed to turn off with the same flick that he'd used to kill the light behind her.

It could have felt like rejection. Except that

Eva was aware of a wash of something that felt like relief.

It would have been impossible to reject that kiss.

And, given how she'd felt in his company this evening—how he'd made her feel that she wasn't a complete failure in her personal life and that she could face any challenge in her life with the kind of support he'd offered—it might have been just as impossible not to fall head over heels in love with this man, and that thought was terrifying because she knew where that could lead.

To broken promises.

To feeling like she wasn't good enough.

To heartbreak and having to try and pick up the pieces and start her life all over again.

Hadn't she already learned the painful lesson that she was happier on her own? Did she really want to go through any of that again?

No...

It was far safer to leave things the way they were and Noa clearly felt the same way.

Maybe he'd even appreciated the prattling, because when she arrived at work the next morning it seemed to have worked.

The reset button had been pushed. Things were back to the way they had been. Better than they had been, in fact, because it felt as if a level of trust had been established. Nobody was going to be pushed into saying, or doing, anything they didn't want to. Boundaries would be respected but there was an understanding that there was something more than a purely professional relationship here.

It might even become a real friendship.

Eva just needed to follow Noa's example and flick the switch on what her body—and possibly her heart—were trying so hard to persuade her was what she actually wanted in her life.

What she needed, even?

CHAPTER SEVEN

EVA DID MANAGE to do exactly that for the next few days, largely helped by having two of those days off where there was no chance of catching even a glimpse of Noa Jones. She also kept herself very busy with her housework, catching up with her family and friends and doing all the rest of her Christmas shopping. The closest she got to sinking into any kind of fantasy involving Noa had been when she spent some very enjoyable time online making a list of websites where he would be able to find everything he could possibly desire to decorate his house.

'Look, this shop had the most beautiful Christmas stockings and, if you're quick, you could get it embroidered with Robin's name on the top. And look at these pretty little wooden ornaments to go on the tree. There are toy soldiers and reindeers and candy canes and gingerbread people and…just *everything*…'

'Haven't I left it too late?'

'No. I checked. If you pay a bit extra, they'll

arrive the same day. When do Robin's grand-parents arrive?'

'The day before Christmas Eve.'

'There you go. You've got plenty of time.'

She did have to bite her lip to stop herself of-fering to help with the task of decorating the house, but changing the subject made it much easier to take the necessary step back. She was doing her best to protect herself here, by tap-ping into the way Noa had constructed such clear boundaries in his life to keep both himself and his son safe.

And talking about Robin was safe ground—a bridge back from anything too personal to some-thing absolutely professional.

'It's starting to look as if he might be able to get home in time for Christmas, isn't it?'

'Fingers crossed.' Noa nodded.

'He's doing so well.' Eva had noticed the dif-ference even a couple of days had made when she was back at work after her days off. 'He can keep his balance walking just by holding onto his IV pole. He doesn't seem to be limping nearly as much, does he?'

'The latest MRI scan was brilliant. The ab-scess is only a fraction of the size it was.'

There was good news about Sheepy the toy, too. It turned out that he hadn't been taken to school but, unexpectedly, Robin had revealed where he'd left his special toy when Eva was reading him a story about farmyard animals.

'I hope Sheepy's had enough grass to eat now,' he'd said.

'Where does Sheepy go to eat grass?'

'In the garden.'

Noa had found the soggy toy half-hidden under a shrub but wasn't going to bring it in until it was clean and dry enough to be cuddled.

Robin wasn't missing the lovey. He was too busy making new friends.

'He wants to have his party in the playroom,' Eva told Noa a day or two later. 'So he can share his cake with everyone.'

The effort to keep her involvement with the arrangements being made to celebrate Robin's birthday to nothing more than she might have done for any other child in her care had been enough to reinforce Eva's determination to get control of any untoward suggestions her body—or heart—might be trying to make her too aware of.

It was all too easy to get too attached to special patients and heartbreak could lie in wait. Sometimes it was devastating, like when a child died. Other times, it was just the ache of missing them for a while when they weren't there to give and receive those cuddles that could fill that hole in her heart. In this particular case, it was especially important. It would be too easy to open her heart to this gorgeous little boy.

Oh, help…she could hear one of those whispers again right now.

And his father…?

Eva felt for that mental switch so she could flick it off yet again.

For her sake. For Noa's sake and for Robin's. The last thing Eva wanted was for Robin to be unhappy when he finally got to go home, because he was missing *her*.

Noa didn't seem to have noticed the effort it had taken to dismiss the wayward thought. Or had it been simply a feeling?

A kind of yearning?

'Sounds like a plan,' he was saying. 'And how are you getting on with that surprise you were planning?'

'Hmm…' Eva made it sound as if the plan was still in progress but it was actually sorted already. She just wanted it to be a surprise for Noa too, because she knew that nothing would make him happier than seeing the joy that she hoped this surprise would give Robin.

Inexplicably, however, that was the day when it felt like something was going very wrong.

Noa should have been as happy as she was that Isla was being discharged this morning and would be able to have Christmas Day with her family at home. Both she and Noa got big hugs from Isla when they were both in her room at the same time to say their goodbyes but Eva could almost feel the way he braced himself for the physical contact from his patient. His smile appeared and was just as gorgeous as ever but there were shadows in his eyes.

Was it because of the angel?

The decoration that Isla had chosen from the box when she was so sick on the day of her admission was still attached to the IV pole on her bed.

'Don't you want to take her home with you?' Eva asked.

'Am I allowed to?' Isla's jaw dropped. 'I thought she had to stay here, to help look after other kids.'

Eva smiled as she shook her head. 'She's your angel. Maybe she can go on your Christmas tree?'

'She could go right on the top,' Kay suggested as she finished packing up Isla's belongings. 'Every Christmas from now on.'

'I think I want her to hang in my room,' Isla said. 'So she can look after me even when it's not Christmas.'

Eva watched Noa walking away from Isla's room moments later. How had he explained to

Robin why he'd never had a mother? she wondered. Had he told him, like some people did, that she was one of the stars in the sky when he looked up on a dark night? Or that she was an angel who could watch over him and help take care of him?

That could certainly explain the cloud that seemed to be hanging over Noa this morning, but it seemed less likely when it hadn't been shaken off by the time Robin was ready to open his birthday presents. He was delighted by the new console and the games to play on it, the books and plastic brick sets that he couldn't wait to get started on, especially the bulldozer, and Noa promised he'd be the first person to play the board game of Snakes and Ladders that had come from his grandparents, but there was something just a little off in Noa's body language that suggested he wasn't feeling the joy.

Nicole coming into the room, along with Robin's physiotherapist, broke what was almost becoming an odd tension.

'Are you free, Noa?'

'Yes. We've about finished unwrapping all these exciting birthday presents. I'm guessing Robin will be very busy for some time putting that bulldozer together.'

'And I don't want any help,' Robin said firmly. 'I can do this all by myself.'

'That's brilliant,' the physiotherapist said. 'I'm going to watch, if that's okay with you, Robin.' The quirk of her eyebrows suggested that the brick-building episode would be great therapy for using his weaker right hand.

'Okay,' Robin said. 'But you're not allowed to help unless I say so.'

'Deal.'

'In that case,' Nicole said, 'I'll steal you for a bit too, Eva. George has just been readmitted and you're the best wrangler of six-year-olds that I've got here today.'

'What's happened?' Noa asked as they followed Nicole.

'He had a seizure at home. Short-lived and he seemed fine when he woke up but after his recent admission for the fainting episodes his parents brought him straight in.'

'Absolutely the right thing to do.' Noa's tone was clipped enough to make Eva think he was remembering that his own son had been admitted for the same reason. It also made him seem like his normal self and that gave Eva a surprising wave of relief.

She hadn't realised how much his apparently low mood had been bothering her.

'His ECG was looking normal in Emergency but Ares thinks he probably needs an EEG, given that a seizure is a step up from the faints. He contacted Cardiology as well, to query getting an ambulatory ECG monitor on him, but they're flat-out at the moment. It might be tomorrow morning by the time they've got a technician free.'

'I know how to put them on,' Eva said. 'I did some work with the cardiology technicians for a while in London.'

'Good.' Noa's nod was approving. 'I'll go and get what we need for a forty-eight-hour recording while you stay and help wrangle George while Neurology is doing an EEG.'

He came back with all the supplies Eva needed to attach a monitor to George that would record his heart rate and rhythm for the next couple of days.

'See this?' She held up a small device as flat as a mobile phone.

'Yes.'

'This is going to record what your heart's doing.'

'Why?'

'Because sometimes hearts don't do what they're supposed to do.'

'What are they supposed to do?'

'They go lub-dub, lub-dub, lub-dub and send blood all round your body.'

'What does mine do?'

'That's what we what to find out. It might be

going lubby-lubby-lubby for a while and making you feel dizzy or even fall over.'

There was a chuckle from Noa's direction. 'That's pretty much what I learned in med school,' he said to George's mother.

'I'm going to stick some electrodes on your chest now,' Eva told Goerge. 'It doesn't hurt. You've had electrodes stuck on before, remember? The last time you were here.'

'Yes.' George wasn't meeting Eva's gaze.

'What did you do with them?'

He put his chin on his chest. 'I pulled them off,' he muttered.

'Mmm…' Eva was cleaning patches of the skin on the small chest with an alcohol wipe as she was talking to him. She was sounding thoughtful now. 'Have you been to see Father Christmas yet, George?' she asked.

'No. We were going to go today.' George's face fell. 'He won't know what I want for Christmas if I don't get to see him, will he?'

'I'll tell you a secret,' Eva said. 'He comes to visit all the kids in hospital too.'

'Does he?'

'He does,' Noa confirmed. 'And do you know what he's going to ask you?'

'Yes…' George gave an audible sigh this time.

'What is it?'

'If I've been good.'

Eva leaned closer to speak to George in a whisper. 'I'm going to tell him how good you've been if you don't pull any of these electrodes off,' she said.

The twitch of Noa's lips into an almost smile made Eva think that whatever had been upsetting him was done and dusted. She was smiling herself as she stuck the electrodes on each side of George's chest and another one in the middle. She put a stretchy belt designed for small children around his waist and slipped the monitor into a pocket on the belt when she had programmed it and started it recording.

'No bath or shower while he's wearing the monitor,' she told George's mother. 'I know he's not going to pull any electrodes off.' They shared a glance as George shook his head to confirm the statement. 'But if one happens to come off accidentally, I'm leaving a supply over here, by the basin. Call me or another nurse and we can help put it back on. There's a diary to write in too, in case George gets any symptoms like feeling dizzy or if he's doing something like going for a walk or playing.'

Noa caught Eva's gaze. They both knew that the more normal activities George did while he was wearing the monitor, the more likely it was they would be able to catch any irregularities that were happening.

'Would you like to go to a birthday party this afternoon, George?'

George nodded happily.

'Who's having a party?' his mother asked.

'My son, Robin,' Noa said. 'And everyone's welcome.'

The distraction of focusing on the admission of a new patient seemed to have worn off by the time Robin's party was in full swing in the playroom, with George there amongst others—including Noa.

Or was it the surprise that Eva had arranged that was making it feel as if Noa wasn't entirely present even though he was in the playroom with everybody else? Had Eva gone too far and was creating a problem because this was something that Robin wanted, but wasn't going to get, for Christmas?

Eva had a friend, Maisie, who had a therapy dog, a gorgeous border collie called Molly, who was a frequent visitor to the hospital and especially this ward but had been out of action for the last few months because she was becoming a mother. The puppies were now six weeks old and totally adorable, and Eva had arranged for Maisie to bring Molly and two of the pups in to take part in Robin's fourth birthday party. A baby's playpen had been set up to keep the puppies safe and Maisie would hold them up to let the children pat them. Robin, however, was allowed to sit inside the playpen and have all the puppy cuddles he could want, with Molly sitting right beside him, keeping an eye on her offspring's behaviour.

Eva was protecting his IV line from sharp puppy teeth but, even at this age, the intelligent little dogs were more interested in licking Robin's face or chewing his slippers than being too boisterous. She'd never seen Robin quite this happy or heard him laughing this much.

'Come and play with them, Daddy.'

'I'm taking some photos,' Noa said. 'Smile...'

He took photos of the cake being shared too, but didn't eat any himself. And then, when Maisie was taking Molly and the puppies home and the children were getting tired, he walked past her and muttered something about needing to go home.

He paused to ruffle Robin's hair and give him a kiss but then he simply kept on walking.

CHAPTER EIGHT

NOA HADN'T RETURNED by the time Eva had Robin settled back in his room, happily playing with a game on his console that involved popping a lot of bubbles.

What was taking so long?

Why had he been acting as if something was wrong all day?

Did it have something to do with *her*? Was Noa angry that she'd fuelled Robin's desire for a puppy by giving him that surprise?

No. Something had been off long before then.

Had she crossed those personal boundaries in other ways as well?

Yeah…she had, hadn't she? More than once. She'd tried to look after him when he was having a tough time after Robin was rushed into hospital. She'd cried on his shoulder about her failure of a marriage. She'd been into his home, and maybe the biggest infraction had been that she would have more than happily kissed him if he'd wanted her to.

Had it been too obvious that *she* wanted to kiss *him*?

When you added it all up, she had done more than simply step over boundaries. She'd had gone too far into a space that Noa Jones had always kept as private as possible.

He wasn't back by the time Eva's shift had finished but she couldn't leave a now sleeping Robin to wake up and find his dad wasn't there. She was glad she had stayed when Robin did wake up and the first thing he did was to call out for Noa.

'He's not back yet, sweetheart.'

'Where did he go?' It was the closest to a whine she'd ever heard from Robin.

'Home.' Without thinking, Eva said the first thing that came into her mind. 'Maybe he's gone to get Sheepy because he's dry now.'

Robin burst into tears.

'I want Sheepy,' he sobbed.

Eva took the little boy into her arms. 'I know. It's okay… Daddy will be back soon.'

'With Sheepy?'

'Yes.'

She needed to contact Noa and make sure he did remember to bring the toy. But she couldn't leave yet, while Robin was so upset. He didn't seem unwell in any way, just overtired after an exciting day, so it wasn't surprising that he fell asleep again a short time later. She tucked him back under his blankets and stroked his hair.

'Sweet dreams,' she whispered. 'I'm going to go and see if I can find where Daddy's got to.'

'And Sheepy?' It was no more than a mumble.

'And Sheepy.'

'Promise…?' He barely finished the word as he sank back into sleep, but Eva answered him anyway.

'I promise.'

It was only a ten-minute walk away but Eva made sure the nurse looking after Robin was going to keep a close eye on him. She didn't bother changing out of her scrubs but put her anorak on, along with a scarf and gloves and her favourite red woolly hat with its shiny silver stars.

She walked fast and didn't let herself wonder whether turning up on Noa's doorstep uninvited would be the worst thing she could do when it came to crossing personal boundaries.

She felt responsible that she had been the one to remind Robin of the comfort of his favourite toy that he'd been missing. Maybe one of the only links he had to a mother he'd never known. If there was some reason why Noa didn't want to be in the hospital at the moment, she would be happy to take the time herself, before she finally went home, to go back and deliver the toy to where it was needed.

This wasn't entirely about keeping her promise to try and ensure Robin got the comfort of his special toy sooner rather than later, however.

This was about Noa.

Because Eva knew something was wrong and the pull to try and help him was, quite simply, overwhelming.

It felt exactly like the time Eva had tapped on the door of the on-call room when there was no response to her knock on the door of Noa's house.

It was cold. And getting damp. When Eva looked up at the streetlamp there was a swirl of white flakes that told her this was sleet that was falling, which didn't surprise her at all. She was starting to lose feeling in her toes. Stooping, she pushed the brass flap of the letterbox and peered inside. The light was on in the hallway and, while she couldn't see through any of the doors or up the stairs, it felt as if the rest of house was dark.

And silent.

Was Noa even here?

If he was, had he fallen asleep? Or worse, slipped on damp, mossy stones out on the patio perhaps and was lying unconscious with a head injury?

Eva pulled off a glove and tried the door handle even though she didn't expect the door to be unlocked. But the big brass knob turned in her hand and the door quietly swung open.

Her heart hammering, Eva went inside and shut the door behind her.

'Noa?' she called softly. 'Are you here? Are you okay?'

She was walking as she called and she'd reached the door to the first lounge—the one with the big fireplace and the ornate ceiling rose for the central light. The room was dark. Eva might have turned and gone upstairs to see if Noa was asleep in his own bed, which seemed more likely, but then she heard it.

A ragged intake of breath.

Almost a snuffle.

As though someone had been crying enough to be so drained they couldn't produce any coherent sound.

Eva's eyes were adjusting to the lack of light. She could see a big pile of unopened boxes in the room and, lying beside them, a Christmas tree that had been delivered with its branches wrapped and tied into a manageable bundle.

She could also see the shape of the man sitting on the couch.

Eva didn't say anything for a long moment. Noa would have heard her calling when she'd come into the house so he knew that it was her and why she was here. Slowly, she pulled off her hat and gloves and unwound her scarf. The central heating was on in the house so this room was warm but there was a chill that had nothing to do with the ambient temperature.

She was holding them as she moved closer to the couch. 'What can I do?' she asked softly. 'How can I help?'

Noa shook his head, a slow roll from one side to the other.

'Nothing.' The word was raw. Then she heard the effort with which he took a new breath. 'Is Robbie okay?'

'He's asleep but…he was asking for you a while ago and…and I didn't think and I told him you might have gone home to get Sheepy and that upset him. I'm sorry… I stayed with him and gave him a cuddle till he went back to sleep and then I… I got worried about you. I thought something might be wrong…'

Noa's breath came out in a sigh. 'It's always a double-edged sword,' he said. 'But I didn't re-alise how hard it would be to have Robbie in hospital—in the *Royal*—for his birthday.' He looked up and met Eva's gaze for the first time since she'd arrived. 'The last time was the day he was born. The day his mother died.' His voice caught. 'Four years ago today. The closer I got to the actual time of day, the harder it was and… I just had to walk away. I'm sorry.'

'Oh, my God, Noa…there's nothing to apologise for.' The items of clothing Eva was holding fell from her hands. She found herself crouching in front of Noa so that she could reach for the hands he had knotted together on his knees on top of what looked like a scrap of sheepskin. Was that Sheepy? 'It's *me* who's sorry,' she said, 'that you felt you had to cope with that alone.'

'I walked out on my son. During his birthday party.'

'You were taking care of him. You didn't want him to see that you were upset—that there's anything sad that associated with him being born.'

'Story of my life,' Noa murmured. 'Balancing what Robbie needs from me as his only parent with what I'm capable of doing. Or being. I never feel like I quite get it right. How can anyone be both a mother and a father to their child? Or be everywhere they need to be at the same time?'

'You're doing a great job,' Eva told him. 'Robin's an adorable, happy little kid who totally adores you. And you're not only a fantastic dad, but you're helping countless other parents—and children—by doing the job you do so amazingly well. You are doing more than most people could and…you deserve to get looked after yourself as well.' She gave his hands a squeeze and stood up again, trying to make this sound as if it was no big deal. That this was just something any friends might do for each other.

'Right…' Eva peeled off her anorak. 'Can I make you a cup of tea? Or do you have some wine in the house? Neither of us are on duty or on call. I expect Robin's out for the count now but I told his nurse to call if he wakes up. He's had a very exciting and exhausting day.' Her smile felt slightly wobbly. 'Playing with puppies can be a bit much, can't it?'

She was rewarded by the slightest quirk of one side of Noa's mouth. 'I don't think I've ever seen him quite that happy. You made a wish come true.' He pulled in a breath. 'There's a wine rack in the kitchen by the back door. Pick anything you like. Even the white ones should be cold enough with where they are.

Eva turned on a lamp rather than flooding the room with light from the chandelier that hung from the ceiling rose. She found a bottle of rosé, which seemed like a good compromise between red and white, took the cork out and opened cupboards until she found some wine glasses. When she went back to the lounge, she found Noa kneeling on the thick rug in front of that big fireplace. She hadn't noticed before that it had an insert of realistic-looking logs that were being licked by gas-fuelled flames—a fireplace with all the charm of an open fire but none of the mess or piles of wood needed.

She knelt on the rug, too. She poured wine into the glasses, put the bottle on the hearth and then sat cross-legged, passing the other glass to Noa.

He leaned back against the sofa and held up his glass.

'Cheers.' He shook his head. 'It's just as well you came by. I had no idea at all how long I'd been sitting there. Me and Sheepy.'

He reached behind him and picked up what had looked like a piece of sheepskin. Eva could see now the flat rectangle and short legs and four hoofy feet attached to it and a floppy head with leather ears that looked…kind of chewed.

'He's seen better days,' Noa admitted. 'But he's been around and well-loved for four years now… He's the last toy Sara bought for Robbie before she died. She'd gone shopping that morning and it was my afternoon off and we'd both been decorating the Christmas tree and laughing about the empty sheep toy. And then she said she wanted to go back into the city and hear the carol singers who were going to be in The Shambles.'

Eva didn't say anything. She knew this story was nowhere near finished and just being here, listening, was probably the best thing she could do for Noa. She took another sip of her wine and simply nodded.

A smile was tugging at the corners of Noa's mouth as he also tasted his wine. 'Sara loved Christmas almost as much as you do,' he said. 'If she'd been a nurse, she would have been right into those festive scrubs you wear and the silly headbands.' He reached out to touch the sleeve of the scrub tunic Eva had on today—a bright red background printed with Christmas trees and brightly wrapped gifts. 'But she worked in a stuffy office in the centre of Birmingham,' Noa added. 'That was how we met—in a coffee shop beside where she worked. I'd just moved there and was out exploring the city.'

The change of tone in his voice made Eva smile. 'You sound like it was love at first sight.'

'I guess it was. Neither of us was in love with Birmingham, though. We went to New Zealand to get married because that was where I grew up and we had our honeymoon in Samoa because that was where my mum grew up and then we came back to the UK...'

'Because that was where Sara had grown up?'

'Yes. And I'm half English on my dad's side.'

'Did Sara grow up in York?'

'No, but she came with me when I had a job interview at the Royal and we walked the city walls and went through the Museum Gardens and along The Shambles and we just knew this was where we wanted to be for the rest of our lives. We bought this house and then Sara got pregnant and…and life was pretty much perfect…' Noa's voice was trailing away. 'Until it wasn't.'

'I'm so sorry,' Eva whispered.

'It was my fault.'

'I don't believe that.'

'It kind of was. We set off to see those carol singers and I got a phone call and I didn't think twice about taking it because I was worried about a kid I'd transferred to the PICU the day before. Sara was looking at me as I answered the call and I knew she didn't want me to be taking a work call while we were out together but I did it anyway.' His voice was almost a whisper. 'So she wasn't watching where she was walking and she stepped too close to the kerb and turned her ankle. She fell into the path of an oncoming car.'

'Oh, my God…' Eva's words were inaudible.

'She was barely alive by the time we got her into Emergency. When she went into cardiac arrest there was no way to even do CPR because of the chest trauma. I don't even remember whether I had any input into the decision to do the perimortem Caesarean. It's a blur. I just remember hearing Robin cry for the first time behind me just when someone was announcing Sara's time of death.'

The sight of tears trickling down the side of

Noa's nose was Eva's undoing as her heart was gripped so hard it hurt. She was moving without thinking of anything other than providing the kind of comfort that only the touch of another human could bestow.

A touch that could make you feel you weren't alone.

Just a hug would be enough.

Oh...

How long had it been since he'd felt the arms of anyone other than a small child around him?

This was being held by someone who understood the devastating blows that life could hit you with.

Someone who understood better than most, in fact, because she'd been through her own challenges in life.

The warmth of her was such a contrast to how cold and alone he'd felt, sitting in here in the dark, not even aware of how much time was passing. He could feel her heart beating against his and the puff of her breath against the skin of his neck. He could smell the scent of her skin and...

...and this was *Eva*. The woman who'd chosen to be with him when Robin was in surgery because that was how much she cared about him, and his son. The woman who'd brought him coffee, and bacon sandwiches and had somehow made it seem okay to go out and do something as silly and fun as riding a wooden horse on a carousel.

The woman who'd looked at him as if she wanted nothing more than to kiss him.

Was that why his hands were threading themselves into the swirl of soft curls that reached her shoulders after brushing tears from her face with his thumbs? Why his gaze was holding hers until the distance between them made it impossible to focus? Why his lips were touching hers?

Just a tentative touch at first. Slow enough to feel the warmth from her mouth and the puff of her breath and…just a hint of what it would taste like to touch her lips with his tongue. And then the pressure deepened ever so slightly and Eva made a tiny sound, like a sigh of need, and Noa felt it echo in every cell of his own body.

And he was lost…

This was his first kiss since he'd felt so numb he'd never have believed he could ever want to kiss another woman for the rest of his life. He hadn't been this close to a woman in…oh, it felt like forever. There was a pent-up need inside him that felt like dynamite and the fuse had just come into contact with a spark that—dammit— he didn't even want to stifle.

He needed this.

As much as he needed to take his next breath.

Eva seemed to be making it very clear by her response to this kiss and his touch that she wanted this as much as he did. He could feel her lips moving beneath his—the tip of her tongue begging for an invitation to taste *him*.

Maybe she needed this just as much as he did? How long had it been since she'd had to face the devastating revelation that her husband wanted another woman more than he wanted her? Since she'd been made to feel as if she wasn't good enough.

Eva Mason was more than good enough.

She was…amazing.

Unbelievably kind. Generous. Sweet enough to make his heart ache and…and so astonishingly sexy that he was completely and utterly lost. His hands found the shape of her body under that baggy, silly scrub top and her skin was soft and silky and he needed to touch it with his lips as well as his hands.

Somehow, they ended up on the rug in front of the fire, naked enough for lovemaking that felt like a release from a prison Noa hadn't realised he'd been trapped inside. Such a release that, in the afterglow, it left him unable to move a muscle. He almost didn't want to take in a new breath because that might break this spell. He wanted to stay like this for ever—with the warmth and softness of this woman in his arms and the sensation that his world had just been turned upside down again, but this time in a good way. A completely unexpected but magically healing kind of way.

It seemed as if Eva didn't want to break the moment in a hurry either. Noa had no idea how long they lay like that because the rules of the real world, including time, were too easy to ignore. Even when his phone started ringing, it took time for the sound to penetrate the bubble they were in. He was almost tempted to ignore the call as well, but that was not something he could do, as either a doctor or a father with a sick child.

Where was the phone?

He spotted it over by the couch, half-hidden by the woolly sheep toy he'd been holding when he was telling Eva about Sara.

The device must have fallen from his pocket when he'd peeled back his jeans that…good grief—he only realised that he hadn't even taken them off completely as he rolled away from Eva and stretched to reach his phone.

He swiped the screen of his phone to answer the call but listened for only a few seconds.

Robin was awake. He was calling for his daddy.

'On my way,' Noa said and then ended the call.

A spark of something like horror was forming as he got to his feet and pulled up his jeans. The sound of the zip closing was like a punctuation mark on what had just happened. Eva was also hastily covering herself with her own clothes. Had he not even thought of protection? He couldn't use the excuse that he knew Eva hadn't been able to get pregnant in the past because he hadn't thought of that either. He hadn't been thinking of anything other than the need for the comfort of Eva's touch and the almost desperate level of desire it had triggered.

Sheepy was still lying on the floor at his feet and the sight of the toy sparked a wave of guilt that was so strong it was shockingly visceral, like a punch in his gut.

He'd sworn he'd never do this.

He had betrayed Sara's memory and there could be no going back from that.

He'd also broken his vow that Robin would always be the most important person in his life. That nobody would ever be allowed to come between them.

He hadn't thought of that either when he'd been swept away by his desire for Eva, and now the worst had happened. His son had woken up to find that his father wasn't where he should be—by his side. On his *birthday…*

Noa stuffed his phone back into his pocket.

He was using the movements as an excuse not to make eye contact with Eva and covering what could have been a very awkward silence with too many words.

'I've got to go,' he said. 'Sorry... Robbie's awake.'

'Is he okay?'

'Apparently. He's just upset that I'm not there. He needs me. Don't feel you need to rush. Or tidy up or anything.' He gestured at the wine glasses abandoned on the hearth as he turned off the fire. 'Have a shower if you want to. I'll set the snib on the front door so you'll just need to pull it closed to lock it when you leave. I... I...'

He *had* to look at Eva. He'd just made love to this woman, there was no way he could walk out of here without acknowledging that. Especially when he could feel her gaze on him.

But it felt like one of the hardest things he'd ever done. Robin needed him. It might take only minutes to get to his son if he ran but it was still going to take too long. He should have been there already. Guilt was closing in on him. About failing his son. Betraying the memory of his wife. Had he also made an unspoken promise to Eva that he wouldn't be able to keep—that the sex meant more than something purely physical? Making that eye contact was going to mix shame with that guilt, wasn't it?

That stack of unopened boxes that he could see behind Eva as he lifted his gaze—the ones that were full of the Christmas decorations he'd ordered online—added yet another layer to the cloak of failure he was pulling around himself.

'Sorry…' It was all he could come up with to say and even that word cracked as he uttered it. 'I shouldn't have let this happen. When Robbie was born, I swore that he would always be my priority. That I'd never let anything come between us. Even something as special as this…' He swallowed hard. '*Especially* something as special as this…'

'It's okay, Noa.' Eva touched his arm. Her eyes were so dark they looked black in this soft light but there was a lightness in her tone that felt like…

Understanding? An acceptance that maybe they both needed to acknowledge that what had happened had been a mistake?

'Go,' Eva added, more firmly. 'Robin needs you.' She stooped to pick something up from the floor. 'Don't forget Sheepy.' She pressed the toy into his hands. 'I promised I'd make sure you remembered.'

And Eva never broke her promises, did she?

Unlike him.

CHAPTER NINE

She'd just made the biggest mistake in her life, hadn't she?

Not because she regretted having sex with Noa Jones.

Quite the opposite.

Eva wouldn't have been able to identify at which moment during that earth-moving experience of lovemaking she'd realised that it wasn't simply that she really liked Noa. Or that he'd awakened a desire that had been dormant since the disappointment of the last date she'd been on, too long ago to be worth remembering. The blinkers had fallen off and she knew, beyond a shadow of any doubt, that she was actually in love with Noa.

Likewise, she wouldn't have been able to pinpoint when she had taken the first step into a space she'd never thought she'd want to be in again. Where she'd peeled off the protective coating around her heart and could imagine gift-wrapping it even, and offering it to someone.

Maybe it had happened during those hours she'd sat with him while Robin was in surgery. Or was it that moment she seen him walking away to be with his son, so staunch and strong—holding hands with that ridiculous, dangling Santa crossed with an elf toy? Perhaps it had been the look in his eyes when he'd made it so clear that he genuinely wanted to know what was upsetting her.

'Talk to me, Eva...'

If she'd been the heroine in some romantic movie, it would have happened when they were on that carousel, on a dark winter's evening, with Christmas lights sparkling like stars all around them and they were simply playing—like a couple of kids who were skipping together, holding hands and smiling at each other.

It didn't matter when it had happened. What mattered—what was probably going to hurt for rather a long time—was that Eva had just destroyed any chance of it ever becoming anything more than a one-sided infatuation by making the stupid mistake of coming here. Worse than turning up uninvited at Noa's home, however, had been to offer him physical comfort that had—possibly inevitably—led to a whole lot more.

On the anniversary of his beloved wife's death. In the very house they'd both lived in.

On the anniversary that was also, horrifically,

the birthdate of the son he'd sworn would always be the most important person in his life.

Eva had made sure he would remember all of that, hadn't she? By shoving the last toy Sara had bought for her unborn baby into his hands.

Had she really thought that she might somehow be able to distract him from the horror of that day? That she might be enough to fill the gaping hole it had left in his life?

There was no getting past it. No matter how Noa had cushioned the rejection by telling her how special she was, it was still the same old story of her life.

She wasn't enough.

Eva did tidy up the wine glasses, washing them and putting them away in the cupboard, because she needed to move before those old ghosts pushed her into a space she really didn't want to be in again. She tipped the rest of the wine into the sink and put the bottle outside in the recycling bin so that when Noa returned home he would have no reminders of what had happened.

She took a slow look around the room before she headed for the front door, to make sure she hadn't left anything behind, like her phone. Her gaze caught as she scanned the rug and she closed her eyes for a moment, to recapture what it had been like lying there in Noa's arms.

It was then that she felt something shift inside her head. And her heart?

The sex might have started as a form of distraction or comfort in an emotionally challenging situation but that wasn't what it had ended up being. Not at all.

That had been lovemaking. The most heartbreakingly tender lovemaking that Eva had ever experienced, and the feeling she'd had being held in his arms afterwards was undeniable. *Real*.

She *was* enough.

Noa simply wasn't ready for another relationship. Maybe he never would be.

She couldn't blame him for the depth of his grief. Or for accepting her offer of comfort tonight. Feeling unwarranted guilt about yet another aspect of his life, thanks to her, would be so unfair it would be unacceptable.

She couldn't do it to him.

She turned out all the lights and made sure the front door was locked behind her. She also made a vow of her own—to make sure that Noa would never know that her heart had been broken tonight.

Because it didn't have to be, did it?

She wasn't going to let this undo all the hard work she'd put into rebuilding her life over such a long time. She had finally reached a space where she knew she could be alone and be happy. She had her family nearby, a wonderful place to live and a job she loved and it was almost her absolutely favourite day of the year.

Nothing had *really* changed.

It would be unreasonable to expect Noa to have changed. He was, in fact, desperately trying to cling to the life he had created after having to start again himself. His focus was always going to be his precious child and the job he was so passionate about.

Perhaps she should just be grateful that she'd been allowed as close as she had become to him. If they could both admit that, due to circumstances, they'd let it go a little too far, maybe it was possible they could put it behind them. And even end up being friends?

She'd know, Eva decided, one way or the other, as soon as she saw him at work tomorrow.

And if it felt at all awkward she would have to try and find a private moment to talk to Noa. To let him know that he had no reason to feel guilty about something that was really no big deal. If she could, she'd want to tell him that he had no reason to feel guilty about the things he'd admitted beating himself up about. Like Sara's accident and his balancing act between his work and his parenting. She would tell him again that he was the best parent that any child could wish for. That she knew he would have been the best husband that Sara could have wished for.

That he was, in fact, someone that deserved the best for himself as well.

Okay…maybe she couldn't tell him that.

But if there was any way she could make this easier, for both of them, she had to try.

The reclining chair in Robin's room couldn't take the entire blame for such a poor night's sleep for Noa Jones.

He finished the shower he was taking in the staff locker room with a blast of cold water, ostensibly to wake himself up properly but it might have also been an unconscious form of punishment.

He'd dragged Eva into the innermost mess of his own life and he'd never intended to inflict that on anyone. He needed to apologise. It was his fault that things had gone too far. He needed to promise that he would never let that happen again.

How awkward was it going to be to work together today?

And how could he even begin to solve the problem that had been created when it was quite apparent that he *was* the problem? Anyone else would have considered himself to be the luckiest man on earth to have been allowed close enough to make love to Eva Mason but here he was, racked with guilt that was threatening to undermine the life he'd built for himself and his son—a life that was as happy as he could have ever expected it to be again.

It was nearly shift changeover time. Noa needed to go back to Robin's room so that Bella, who'd been writing up notes from overnight and recording the early set of vital signs, could get to the handover meeting that would be happening any minute. He left the locker room and walked along a corridor that was still dark enough for the coloured lights on the Christmas tree beside the reception desk to be providing a blurry kaleidoscope on the wall beside him and it was then that he saw Eva.

His breath caught and his good intentions to make that promise that last night would never happen again was taking a hit, thanks to being ambushed by a feeling that it was something else entirely that he should be apologising for. That he hadn't been able to stay longer? To keep holding her in his arms and to tell her how utterly amazing a person she was?

But Eva wasn't smiling. She wasn't even looking at him.

'Have you seen George? He's not in his room.'

'No, I was having a shower.'

Nicole came out of the main patients' bath-

room. 'He's not in here. I can't see his mum anywhere either.'

'She went home,' Eva said. 'She's got two-
year-old twins and her husband's just come down
with that bug that's going around.'

'I'll check out by the lifts. We'll have to alert
Security if we don't find him in the next few
minutes.'

'I'll see if he's gone to visit Robin,' Noa offered. 'They seemed to be making great friends
when they were playing with those puppies at
his birthday party yesterday.'

'Oh…maybe he's gone back to the playroom,
then. I'll go there.'

Noa had just reached the door of Robin's room
when he heard the call.

'*Help…* I need some help here. And a crash
cart.'

Eva's voice. Loud and clear but still calm.

Noa ran through the playroom door only seconds later to see Eva kneeling beside the limp
form of a small boy.

'George… *George…* Can you hear me?' She
was holding his shoulders and giving him a
shake.

Noa could see that there wasn't even a hint of
response. He dropped to his knees on the other
side of the unconscious child. He put his finger

on George's chin and pushed to open his mouth so he could glance inside.

'No sign of any foreign body.'

It was safe to tilt the back and lift the chin to make sure the airway was open. Eva was unbuttoning his pyjama jacket. The electrodes and wires for the Holter monitor he was wearing were attached to the electronic device on a belt.

'Take it off,' Noa instructed.

Nicole was rushing into the area pushing a crash cart.

'Throw me an OPA,' Noa said. 'And can you get the monitor to Cardiology for an urgent analysis?'

'Sure.'

Nicole took the device from Eva and ran from the room, pausing for only a millisecond to hit the red cardiac arrest button on the wall to summon extra help.

Noa slipped the plastic oropharyngeal airway into George's mouth as a temporary protection for his airway. It was still only seconds since they'd found him and now he could take the ten seconds needed to look, listen and feel for any signs of breathing. His fingers were pressed into the neck to feel for a carotid pulse at the same time.

A small, six-year-old boy's neck.

About the same size as Robin's would be, but

Noa couldn't afford to think of anything like that. This was serious.

As serious as it got.

'No pulse, no respiration.' His words were curt. 'I'm starting CPR.' He put the heel of one hand onto the centre of the chest Eva had exposed, which was now clear of the electrodes and wires. 'Find a bag mask for me, would you, please, Eva, and get some pads on.'

She was assessing the child's size too, as she opened the packs to take out the defibrillation pads. 'Front and back placement or anterior lateral?'

Noa was counting in his head. He wanted a hundred compressions a minute and a rate of fifteen to two for breaths but it was automatic enough for him to be able to respond to Eva.

'I think he's big enough for anterior lateral.'

She worked around his movements as he kept up the compressions and stopped only briefly to fit the face mask and hold it tightly to cover both the mouth and nose of George's face as he squeezed the bag. He liked that he didn't have to tell Eva to attach the tubing to the oxygen cylinder attached to the crash cart and turn on the flow. Or to turn on the defibrillator after she'd swiftly clipped the electrodes to the pins on the sticky pad that had now been stuck under the right clavicle and on the lower left-hand side of the chest.

Noa paused compressions just long enough to analyse the rhythm now showing on the screen of the defibrillator.

'V-fib.' The words were almost a groan. 'And fine. I think he's been down for a while.'

Ventricular fibrillation was a fatal rhythm that made a wiggling line on the ECG trace. If the cardiac arrest had only just happened, the size of the wiggle would be considered coarse because it was wider. The wider it was, the more chance they had of correcting it. A fine line was getting closer and closer to a flat line and you couldn't defibrillate a flat line.

'Charge to one hundred joules,' Noa ordered.

Eva hit the button and the crescendo of sound told them the charge was accumulating. They both knew that it was imperative to deliver this first shock as soon as possible. Her finger was poised over the button to deliver the charge as soon as the beeps indicated the target was reached but Noa shared the responsibility to do the safety checks.

'Stand clear,' he said. He sat back on his heels, holding his hands up in the air, looking around as he did so for anything on the floor that could conduct electricity.

'Clear,' Eva confirmed, for herself and Noa.

There was no one else in the room as the first shock made George's body jerk.

'Take over compressions, please, Eva.' Noa opened a drawer on the crash cart. 'I'm going to prep for intubation.'

There was no way in the world that Eva was thinking of anything other than this fight to bring back a little boy who was still lying life-less between herself and Noa.

Other people were arriving now. Nicole was back, along with other ward staff and the cardiac arrest crew summoned by sounding the alarm were setting up their gear, including a portable ventilator that would take over supplying oxygen and a device that could provide the chest com-pressions to deliver that oxygen by keeping the blood circulating.

It felt as if the spotlight was still on Noa, how-ever, as he positioned George's head into a 'sniff-ing' position, removed the plastic tube that had been holding his airway open and slipped the curved blade of a laryngoscope into his mouth instead.

'ET tube, uncuffed, size five point five,' he requested. 'And draw up some adrenaline and amiodarone. We'll need intraosseous IV access during the next rhythm check as soon as he's intubated.'

How Noa was managing to make this look like a smooth process when Eva was still doing compressions that had to be making this a very difficult procedure was astonishing. She knew that the guidelines stated compressions couldn't be stopped for more than five seconds during a paediatric resuscitation, which was why nobody was hovering to take over her task, but that would change with the next rhythm check. And Noa was not only managing to insert a breathing tube in a moving trachea, he was thinking ahead to everything else that could be done to save this young life.

Eva sent up a silent plea to the universe that the rhythm would still be shockable when they paused for the next check. If only she'd found George earlier. If only he'd had an implantable defibrillator nestled inside his own body so that a small shock could have been delivered the moment his heart had stopped functioning normally.

Syringes of drugs were drawn up, double-checked and labelled, ready for administration after the second shock was delivered. Someone was standing behind Eva, ready to take over compressions. The whine of the defibrillator charging again was all she could hear.

'Stand clear.'

For a split second, Noa's gaze caught Eva's after he'd watched to make sure she had lifted her hand from George's chest and no other part of her body was in contact. It was a vital element to this resuscitation protocol but somewhere, in the back of her mind, it felt as if she was being protected on more than a professional level.

That the fight for George's life on Noa's part was also on a very personal level as well. Noa's passion for his work and the focus and skill he brought to it was second to none. For that tiny moment of time, as Eva held her breath and watched George's body respond to the jolt of electricity that was aimed to go straight through his heart, she had never felt so proud of anyone as she did of Noa Jones.

There was just as much love mixed in with that feeling, so perhaps it wasn't surprising that her eyes filled with tears as she saw the blip of movement on the screen of the defibrillator, followed immediately by another blip and then a shape that told them George's heart was doing what it was supposed to do to keep him alive.

The crisis wasn't over yet, but Eva's part in it was.

She moved out of the way as the ventilator was hooked up because George hadn't started breathing effectively for himself yet. The intraosseous device that would be much faster to place than a cannula that went into a small flat vein, to deliver IV medications was screwed into position in a leg bone and attached to a bag of fluids. A bed was brought in and people went to hold doors open and clear corridors so that they could get George into the intensive care unit as soon as possible.

Noa went with him, of course.

Eva stayed behind. She would go to Robin and explain why he might not see his dad for a while because he was busy helping another little boy who was very sick. George's mother was probably already on her way to the hospital and if she was lucky enough to find that her son had survived a cardiac arrest without serious complications, a plan would have to be put into place to make sure that this didn't happen again.

Eva was unlikely to get any time to speak privately to Noa. Even if she did, talking about what had happened between them last night would be entirely inappropriate.

Telling him how proud she was of him would also be a mistake.

Giving him even a glimpse of how she felt about him would be worse than saying nothing at all because she knew how big a heart this man had. How deeply he was capable of loving others, and if he thought she'd been hurt by anything he'd done—or wasn't able to do—she would be contributing to the guilt and grief that was already a burden he didn't deserve to be carrying. She'd already acknowledged how unfair it would be to do that.

She needed to find a way around this that would make it easier for both of them, and maybe the best thing Eva could do for the rest of her shift was to make sure she avoided being too close to Noa Jones at all.

Nicole, unwittingly, managed to make things a whole lot easier.

'We've got two more staff members down with flu,' she told Eva. 'I'm getting desperate. Too many people can't come in because they're travelling out of town to see family or need to be with their own kids. Can I ask a huge favour, Eva?'

'What's that?'

'I can get someone in for tomorrow before they head off, so if you could have your day off then and cover the morning shift on Christmas Eve and then be on standby for Christmas Day, I will be eternally grateful.'

Eva might have family but she was one of the few that didn't have her own children and she'd often covered Christmas Day for that very reason. Her own family might be disappointed but they would understand.

It also meant that it would only be for the rest of today's shift that Eva would have the tension of knowing she could bump into Noa at any point. There was already discussion about Robin being discharged to be home in time for Christmas and Eva knew that Noa would be taking time off, not only to look after his son but to celebrate a family Christmas with his parents, who were arriving from New Zealand tomorrow.

Her time of sharing the life of Noa's family was all but over.

She might not even see him over the next week or more.

The new year would be beginning by then and maybe the best thing Eva could do was to wrap up the last few weeks of this year into a memory she would treasure for ever.

She could get on with her own life with a new year and a new start.

She could actually start tomorrow because she now had the opportunity to finish any last-minute Christmas preparations. With a bit of luck, she would be able to arrange an early family celebration with her family, given that this change in her shifts would disrupt the original plans they'd made.

Eva wasn't going to let that dampen the joy of Christmas. She would invent a new event to exchange gifts and call it…um…

Maybe…the day before the day before Christmas. Christmas Eva?

It would still be a happy family occasion because Eva would make sure of that.

She knew she might need every bit of joy that she could create right now.

CHAPTER TEN

SOME DAYS WERE more exhausting than others—
it was simply a part of life.

Occasionally, however, there was a day that
absolutely flattened Noa and today had been one
of those.

It hadn't helped that it had started with his
head all over the place after last night and his already messy life having been shaken up enough
to feel like a train crash.

Not that it had interfered in the slightest with
his focus and determination to succeed in the
resuscitation of a small boy who reminded him,
too much, of his own son. Running that cardiac
arrest scenario and being there until George was
stabilised in the ICU had used up enough adrenaline to leave him even more drained, but that
hadn't been the end of it by any means.

He had to sit down with George's parents and
explain what had happened later that morning.

'We don't know why he'd gone into the playroom by himself. It could be that he remem-

bered all the excitement from yesterday when we had some puppies in there for the children to play with.'

'He does love dogs...' George's mother had to reach for a new handful of tissues. 'He's been asking Father Christmas for a puppy every year but I said we had to wait until the twins were older because...you know...it would have been too much.' She burst into tears again. 'And now it might be too late...'

Noa could feel an echo of this parent's fear for their child. He'd felt it himself that day in the emergency department of the Royal, when Robin was lying on the bed and he was beginning to realise how sick his son was. He could hear an echo of Robin's voice as well. And Eva's.

'Have you written a letter to Santa, sweetheart? To tell him what you want for Christmas?... Do you know what you want?'

'Mmm...'

'What is it?'

'A puppy...'

'But *how* did it happen?' The angry note in George's father's voice drowned those echoes. 'How can a kid's heart just suddenly stop?'

The cardiologist looking after George had already explained this but Noa patiently went over it again.

'It's the same reason that causes the kind of

fainting episodes that George has had. And that seizure, because his heart had stopped long enough for him to be too short of oxygen. With Long QT syndrome, the heart can just kick back into a normal rhythm by itself but it can also tip into what's called ventricular fibrillation and that needs a shock to make it revert.'

'But *how*…? He's such a fit kid. Always running around and full of energy.' There were tears rolling down the young father's face now. 'I don't understand.'

'In simple terms,' Noa said carefully, 'when a heart beats, it needs a little bit of time to get ready for the next beat. If a new beat happens before it's ready, it can disrupt the normal rhythm and sometimes it can't recover without help.'

'But he's going to be okay, isn't he?'

'He's doing well. We're going to wake him up again soon.'

'And what happens then?'

'Then we'll talk about what we can do to make sure it doesn't happen again. We can implant a small device that will monitor his heartbeat and can give him a shock if it's needed—even if he's asleep or there's no one else around.'

'What about the twins? Are they in danger too?'

'We'll need to arrange testing for everybody in the family.'

'When will you wake George up? When will we know if he's…' The words couldn't be said. Nobody wanted to think about the possibility that George might have been without oxygen for long enough to suffer serious brain damage.

They didn't need to. Part of today's roller-coaster had been the enormous relief of taking George off the ventilator and finding he could breathe well for himself. Watching him wake up and hold out his arms to his mother for a cuddle the instant he recognised her.

'*Mummy*…'

Time was needed to explain the procedure of implanting an internal cardioverter defibrillator, which would be done as soon as possible under a general anaesthetic. Until then, George would have to stay in bed, hooked up to a monitor that would warn them instantly if his heart slipped into a dangerous rhythm again. George also needed to be prepared for what could be a scary experience, but it rapidly became clear that he was more interested in hearing about the sleigh bed that he would get to ride in. Noa had seen the bed many times, ferrying children to and from the theatre suite. Until now, it had only been part of the background decorations of a season he preferred to ignore, but the way George's eyes lit up was a very poignant reminder that this morning's drama could have had a very different outcome.

Thank goodness Eva had found George when she did.

'Just for me?' he asked. 'I get my own Christmas sleigh?'

'Just for you.' Noa smiled. 'Because you're special.'

Finally, he was alone with another special little boy.

His precious son.

It was late and Robin was almost asleep, clutching Sheepy under one arm, his cheek pressed against the wool, his fingers rubbing the remains of one of the ears he used to chew when he was younger.

Noa stroked back his hair and placed a gentle kiss on his forehead.

'Sweet dreams, monkey. You might be back in your own bed by Christmas Eve.'

The MRI this afternoon had shown that the abscess was almost gone. He could come off his IV antibiotic regime if the next blood tests were reassuring enough and continue treatment orally from now on. He would still need to be monitored carefully and have some physical therapy, but it looked as though Robin Jones was on his way to a complete recovery.

'And Nana and Grandpa are going to be here tomorrow?'

'Yes. They're in their big aeroplane up in the sky on their way here. They'll have to stop to get some more fuel in Dubai and I think they have a few hours to wait there, and I've heard there are so many shops in that airport it's like the biggest mall in the world.'

'What will they buy?' Robin was trying hard to keep his eyes open now. 'Christmas presents?'

'We'll have to wait and see, won't we? They'll get on another plane after that and land in Manchester, and then they'll rent a car and drive here to York. Right to our front door.'

'And they'll stay for Christmas?'

'Absolutely.' Noa tried not to think of what his parents' expressions might be when they walked through that door and saw piles of boxes instead of the beautifully decorated house he'd imagined. Had he really thought he was capable of sprinkling Christmas magic around as easily as Eva seemed able to do?

'They'll be very tired when they get here because it's such a long way from New Zealand, but they can have a big sleep and then they'll be all ready for Christmas Eve, and that's only one sleep away from Christmas Day.'

'And you're going to be there too?'

'Of course I will.' Oh, help…was Robin afraid

that his work might take him away from his family on such a special day? It was a possibility, wasn't it?

But Noa could hear a whisper of something Eva had said to him last night.

'...*you're not only a fantastic dad, but you're helping countless other parents—and children...*'

'Unless someone else really needs me for a little while,' he added. 'Like George did today.'

'But you'll come back?' Robin's eyes flickered open. 'And be here for ever and ever? Not like Mummy...?'

Noa had to swallow a lump in his throat. Could he make a promise that big when he had no control over what life had in store for him?

'I'm here,' he said softly. 'With you. And I don't want to be anywhere else. I'm going to be right here in this chair when you wake up.'

He watched Robin drift into a deep sleep, a small smile curving one side of his mouth.

He looked...happy.

Exactly the way Sara would have wanted her little boy to be.

She would have loved that he was cuddling Sheepy while he slept.

Only under that one arm, mind you, because Santa-elf was under the other one, but Sara would have smiled at that. She would have been so happy that their son was happy. It was all any parent wanted for their children, after all.

Robin was so excited that his grandparents were coming to visit. And more excited than ever about Christmas this year. Noa remembered the way his whole face had been glowing when he'd taken him down to see the huge Christmas tree by the front door of the Royal.

'I love Christmas trees,' he'd said. And then he'd smiled. *'I love Eva, too.'*

He was so full of love, this child.

So happy.

Just like his mother.

He could feel Sara's presence in this room, partly through her likeness in her son and partly from his own memories of someone he'd loved so much.

He could almost hear a whisper of her voice.

Are you happy, Noa?

He *was* happy. He had his precious son. He had a job he loved. His parents were coming to make it a family Christmas. He had everything he needed.

Except…

The biggest thing he'd lost? The support and comfort of going through life with a partner. Someone who loved him. Someone he loved.

Sara wouldn't have wanted him to go through life alone, but that was what he'd been doing for the last four years and he hadn't thought he was lonely.

Until now.

Until… Eva had slipped into his life. And Robin's life.

Noa leaned forward in his chair, closing his eyes as he rested the weight of his head in his hands—the way he had that day in the waiting room when Robin had been taken into the operating theatre and none of them knew how bad things were yet. He'd wanted to tell Eva not to stay because he was quite capable of coping alone, as he always had. He'd pretty much ignored her but she hadn't deserted him. She'd simply been there.

Supporting him.

Providing the comfort of human company.

A touch like no other he'd ever experienced in his life. Because it had been so long since anyone had touched him like that?

Or was it because of the way he felt about Eva?

That, despite his determination to never let it happen again, he was falling in love with her?

He'd run away from facing that thought last night, hadn't he? He'd dismissed what had happened as no more than a passing physical encounter. He'd effectively dismissed Eva and he knew that must have hurt her. He just didn't know any other way of dealing with the maelstrom of such huge feelings he'd never expected to feel again. He'd seen the confusion in her eyes and felt the way she was stepping back from him. Pushing him away even, by telling him that he had to go. Disguising her own hurt by making it all about what Robin needed?

Had she actually been trying to help him?

To make it easier for him?

She hadn't shown any signs of being hurt this morning, though. Or being angry with him, which she had every right to be. No...she'd been by his side, ready to work with him and pretend that he hadn't pushed her away. Was it possible that she understood that he hadn't been able to cope with the overwhelming emotions that were coming at him from all sides? That his guilt had overridden the comfort that Eva had so unexpectedly given him?

The love...?

It seemed so obvious now.

Getting to know Eva was the biggest gift he could have been given.

He needed her in his life.

Robin needed her in his life.

He'd been battling that rollercoaster for so long now, trying to keep the balance between those two halves of himself as a doctor and as a father. How had he not seen that how difficult it was might be because he was missing something in his life that was just as important to who he was?

The part he'd given up on when he'd lost Sara.

The part that could welcome someone else into his life and into his heart.

The part that could be a best friend. A lover. A husband.

Had he found that missing part of his life in Eva?

But had he messed things up so much he might have lost it already? He wouldn't blame Eva if she didn't want anything more to do with him. She'd come out of a marriage feeling as if she wasn't good enough. He'd walked away from her last night without saying anything that might have stopped her feeling like that all over again.

How on earth could he apologise for that in a way that would be enough?

What would make Eva happy?

As happy as she'd been last night. When she was lying in his arms, her breath mingling with his own and her heart beating against his. Before that damned telephone call had interrupted what had been the happiest moment Noa had experienced for too many years.

As he saw—and *felt*—that moment again in his mind, Noa could also see the pile of boxes that had been around them and the tree that was lying on the floor, tied up like the victim of a crime.

That was what he could do, he decided.

Eva loved Christmas more than anyone he knew.

He could unpack every single one of those boxes and turn his house into the Christmas grotto he'd imagined, with fairy lights everywhere and a tree with a star on the top. His parents would help him. They could light the fire and have delicious food cooking.

He would invite her to join his family for Christmas and that might totally erase the memory Eva must have of seeing him sitting in there alone. In the dark.

Maybe, it might end up being an invitation to join them for more than just a Christmas Day...

CHAPTER ELEVEN

IT WAS BELLA who arrived with the breakfast tray the next morning and Noa saw the way Robin's face fell. The way he blinked suggested that tears might not be far away, in fact.

'Where's Eva?' he asked, his tone anxious. 'She said she had a special Santa hat she was going to wear today.'

'Sorry, sweetie, Eva's not working today after all.'

Noa froze. 'She's not sick, is she?'

'No. But some other nurses are so the roster's been changed a bit. Eva's got a day off today because she'll be working extra time over the next few days instead.'

It should have been a relief in that it would give him extra time to plan what he could say to Eva, but Noa's heart was sinking rapidly. If she wasn't in the hospital, how was he going to find time to talk to her? In a space that was private enough to apologise. How could he invite her to come and spend at least part of her Christmas

Day with him and Robin if she was going to be at work that day?

How on earth was he going to even start trying to fix the mess he'd made?

The horrible thought occurred to him that Eva might have been relieved by the roster change because it meant she wouldn't *have* to see him.

'What's the matter, Daddy?' Robin was staring at him and looking increasingly worried.

'Nothing, monkey. I'm just feeling a bit…hungry, I guess.'

'You can have my egg.'

'That's very kind.' Noa managed to find a smile. 'I might go and make myself some toast while you're having breakfast with Bella.'

'That's a great idea,' Bella said cheerfully. 'What does Daddy have on his toast, Robin? Peanut butter? Marmalade?'

'Sometimes it's jam.' Thankfully, Robin seemed to be distracted from Eva's absence now. 'And sometimes it's peanut butter.'

'Do you know that people in America like to have jam *and* peanut butter on their toast? And in their sandwiches.'

Robin shook his head. 'That's silly.'

Noa grinned. 'I might try it,' he said. 'Tell you what, I'll go and make my toast and come back and we can have breakfast together.'

He'd have to think about finding a way to talk

to Eva later. After breakfast, it would be time for Robin's blood tests and they were particularly significant today. If they were consistent with what had been seen on yesterday's MRI, the IV line could be removed later today and there would be no reason for Robin to stay in hospital any longer. He could be home, possibly in time to be there to greet his grandparents.

The first significant result that came in later than morning, however, was the analysis of George's Holter monitor recording.

Noa met with the cardiology team who had the period of time right before the cardiac arrest printed out onto a long scroll of paper.

'Look at this, Noa. Absolutely classic Torsades de Pointes.'

'It certainly is.' Noa traced the extraordinary heart rhythm with his finger, starting before it changed so dramatically, counting the tiny squares between the different points on the ECG trace—from where the Q wave first dipped into its spike to the end of the hump of the T wave at the end of the cycle.

'Longer than five hundred milliseconds,' he murmured. 'I wonder how often he's had a self-reverting torsades in the past. It was highly likely to be the reason for those fainting episodes and that seizure.'

The fatal rhythm hadn't reverted back to normal this time, however. The dangerously rapid ventricular rhythm turned what should have been regular forms into wild dips and peaks and, notably, they suddenly got smaller as if they were again twisting around the baseline before expanding again. And then it had deteriorated into the wild squiggle that was fibrillation.

This was confirmation that the planned course of treatment to give George an implantable defibrillator was exactly what needed to be done.

'We can do the insertion today,' the cardiologist said. 'We kept him on nil-by-mouth in the hope we could get a slot. We'll put him on prophylactic antibiotics and keep him in for monitoring. I'm not sure we'll get him home in time for Christmas, but his parents are happy to sign the consent forms.'

'They came too close to losing him,' Noa said, his tone sombre. 'Having him alive for Christmas is the best gift they could possibly get, even if he's not at home.' He raised an eyebrow. 'Will you do an abdominal insertion for the generator?'

'Yes. We'll do it in Theatre under a general anaesthetic, put a dual-chamber generator in an upper quadrant and attach the leads to the surface of the heart. The procedure will take anywhere from one to three hours, depending on how long the testing and programming will take.'

'Can I join you?' Noa glanced at his watch. 'I can finish my ward round in the next thirty minutes and I've never seen the procedure, other than on video.'

'Please do.' The cardiologist's smile was a little rueful. 'It's you the parents are hanging out to talk to about all this. They'll be delighted if you're in there, keeping an eye on things. I'll give you the consent forms to go over with them and I can go and get things set up.'

'I'll go and have a chat to them now,' Noa said. 'I'm guessing George will be very happy to know that the sleigh bed will be arriving today.'

Eva saw the red sleigh bed going into a lift as she headed for the stairs that would take her up to the paediatric ward. It was empty but it still made her smile. So did the group of carol singers who were grouped beneath the huge Christmas tree in the foyer, enthusiastically performing everybody's favourite seasonal songs.

She wasn't wearing her Christmas scrubs this morning. She was in her jeans and boots, but was at least wearing a seasonal jumper that was bright red, with a very happy reindeer's face on the front and antlers that went all the way up to her neckline. She wasn't wearing the special hat that she'd told Robin about, however. She had that in her hand because she was going to give it to her favourite patient. She had another gift for him in her bag, just in case he went home before she was back on duty tomorrow—the little robin ornament she'd bought at the market that night that she and Noa had ridden the carousel. The night of that moment that could have turned into a kiss.

Had he found time to unwrap that Christmas tree she'd seen in his house the night they'd done a whole lot more than simply sharing a kiss? Or open any of those boxes that were presumably filled with the decorations he'd ordered online, thanks to all those suggestions she'd provided for him? Eva had her doubts, given that he spent his evenings and nights in Robin's room and how busy he'd been at work yesterday after that dramatic start of George's cardiac arrest and following through his stabilisation and tests.

It didn't matter if the tree wasn't ready, though. That little robin on a twig didn't have to hang from a branch of a Christmas tree, did it? Maybe Robin would like to hang it in his own bedroom or put it on his windowsill. She might even suggest that as an idea, because how wonderful would it be if a real robin came and sat on the outside windowsill to see who was inside? That was a notion that would appeal to any small child.

Her heart was in her mouth as she reached her ward. Would Noa be in with Robin at the moment? Was she ready to see him again yet? The only time she'd had with him yesterday had been during the horribly tense situation of working to resuscitate George but that had, in its own way, been helpful. Personal thoughts about Noa Jones, let alone any private words with him, had been the furthest thing from her mind and, although it had only been a short period of time, it had shown her that it was possible.

Even if they couldn't end up being friends, they would be able to work together and that was so important. Eva couldn't bear to lose the joy she had in a job she loved so much—in the city she also loved, because it was her home.

Nicole was in the reception area of the ward, behind the desk adorned with the string of gingerbread people holding hands. Beside the tree that Eva had decorated herself on the very first day of December.

The day that Robin Jones had been rushed into hospital after his seizure and she was still unaware of how much her world had begun to shift on its axis.

'What on earth are you doing here?' The

charge nurse shook her head. 'You're supposed to be having a day off, remember?'

'I am,' Eva assured her. 'I'm on my way to go shopping. I'm doing an early Christmas dinner with my family this evening in case I'm working on Christmas Day and I'm on my way to the supermarket. I told them I'm making dinner and it's going to be pigs in blankets for the main course and pavlova for dessert. Not a Brussels sprout to be seen. My niece and nephew are delighted.'

Nicole laughed. 'What are you doing in here, then?'

'I forgot to tell Robin I had the day off today. He wanted to see this hat.' She held up the hat, which was a circle of white fluff supporting a red-velvet-covered wire shaped like a giant spring that had a white pompom on the top. 'It bounces. See?' She squashed the coil and it popped up again.

'He'll love it,' Nicole said.

Eva turned to go towards Robin's room but then paused. 'Where's the sleigh bed gone? I saw it going into the lift downstairs.'

'PICU, I expect,' Nicole said. 'George is heading to Theatre to get an ICD implanted.' She smiled at Eva. 'Noa was just saying that you need the credit for finding him when you did.

He's not showing any signs of brain injury from lack of oxygen.'

Eva shook off the praise. 'I think Noa gets the credit more than I do. He was amazing.' She cleared her throat and tried to sound casual. 'Is he in with Robin at the moment?'

Nicole shook her head. 'He's gone to observe in Theatre for the ICD implantation. Could take a couple of hours.'

She should be feeling relieved, Eva told herself as she approached the quiet room at the end of the ward. It was ridiculous to be feeling as if the sun was never going to shine quite as brightly again.

Robin's smile was as bright as ever. 'Bella said you weren't here today.'

'I'm not.' Eva put her finger to her lips. 'It's a secret. Don't tell anybody.'

'I won't.' Robin's gaze had dropped to her hand. 'Is *that* the hat?'

'It is. Look…it bounces.' The pompom bounced as Eva showed him how to push the coil down and then let it go. The sound of his laughter was a balm to her soul.

'It's the best hat ever,' he declared. 'Why aren't you wearing it?'

'Because it's for you to wear.' The white fluff of the circle was slightly big for Robin's head but it didn't matter because his ears stuck out just far enough to stop it falling down too far, even when he nodded his head to make the pompom jiggle.

'Is it really for me?' he asked, his eyes very round.

'It is. Happy Christmas.'

Eva reached for her shoulder bag to find the small tissue-wrapped parcel that contained the real gift she wanted to give this special little boy.

'My nana and grandpa are coming for Christmas,' Robin told her as she opened her bag. 'And I might be going home. Can you come too, Eva?'

Her hands stilled. So did her heart.

How gorgeous would that be?

How impossible would it also be?

'That's so sweet of you,' she said. 'But Christmas is for your family, darling. And I might be working—I don't know yet.'

'But I want you to come.' Robin's bottom lip wobbled. 'Can't you come? *Please?* You could be my mummy—just for Christmas?'

Oh, *no*…

Eva had no way to respond to this. Her mind was racing. She had a flash of seeing that expression on Noa's face as she'd tried to distract Robin when he'd been so distressed in Emergency that day, by asking if he'd written a letter to Father Christmas to say what he was hoping for, and he'd said, *'A puppy…'* and she had known that it was too much for Noa to even contemplate.

He'd said it aloud when she'd suggested that his lovely long garden would be perfect for a dog.

'Don't you start. I've got quite enough on my plate without trying to juggle another family member...'

Imagining what that expression would be if Robin told him now that he wanted 'a mummy' for Christmas was enough to send a chill down Eva's spine. It would be like seeing the rejection in Aaron's eyes when he'd told her that their marriage was over. Only it would be worse because it would be a rejection as a potential mother as well as a family member. And there would be an apology in his face too, because he would know how much it would hurt Eva to know that she wasn't wanted—or needed—as even a temporary, *pretend* mother.

Robin only knew his mother through his dad keeping her memory alive but she was very much still a treasured member of their family and that was something Eva could never dream of being because Noa wanted to keep his life exactly the way it was.

Stepping into that gap in their lives just for a little while—for Christmas—was the worst thing she could possibly do.

Because Noa would hate it but he might pretend otherwise, for Robin's sake.

Because Eva would love it because that had always been the dream, hadn't it?

A family.

And Christmas Day was all about family.

That was why she couldn't do it, even for Robin's sake. Because she might not be able to pretend it wasn't breaking her heart.

If Robin suggested it to his father, it could make it very difficult for Eva to be able to work with Noa. He might find it unforgivable that she'd got close enough to his son to intrude on the space reserved in their lives for his real mother.

Or that she'd got as close as she had to *him*. She might even see regret in his eyes that they'd made love that night.

But how could she explain any of that to a four-year-old boy who was holding his arms out to her with absolute confidence that she would return his love?

She couldn't say a word. All she could do was cuddle him. And give him kisses. And to hope that would be enough to let him know he *was* loved, but also an apology for not being able to step out of her professional boundaries and love him in the real world.

She also had to get out of here as fast as possible. Before Noa could come back.

'I've got to go, sweetheart,' she whispered into

Robin's ear. 'You keep that hat on and have the best, bounciest Christmas ever.'

It was only when she was out of the room and halfway down the stairs that Eva realised she'd totally forgotten to give him the robin ornament. But there was no way she could go back.

She wanted to be as far away from the hospital as possible before she started crying…

CHAPTER TWELVE

IT WAS A rare treat to be involved in something out of the ordinary like being invited into Theatre to watch the implantation of an implantable cardioverter-defibrillator. Noa didn't need to scrub in but he did need to wear a gown, shoe covers, hat and a mask in this sterile environment and while he was getting himself ready he realised he wasn't quite absorbed by this new experience yet.

He was still aware of being as disappointed as Robin had been when he'd learned that Eva wasn't at work today. Part of his brain was still trying to come up with a plan to talk to her, but how could he if she wasn't anywhere near the hospital? He didn't know where she lived. It felt like he needed to do it face-to-face. It might be too easy for her to say 'no' if he texted or called her.

It would have to wait. George had been given his general anaesthetic in the anteroom and was now being wheeled into Theatre. For the next couple of hours, Noa's focus was going to be exactly where it should be—captured by the fascination in a process of being able to implant a small device that contained life-saving technology for a child who could so easily die without it.

He watched the care that the paediatric cardiac surgeon was taking to nestle the titanium casing that was about the size of a stopwatch beneath the rectus muscle of George's abdomen. Inside was the tiny computer and a battery that should last about ten years but would be checked at regular intervals. The wires that carried the electrical charge if and when it was needed were stitched carefully to the surface of the child's small heart.

'With the kind of advances being made in this technology,' the surgeon told Noa, 'it could well be that he'll get a subcutaneous replacement when he's a bit older that will be completely wireless.'

Now that the device was in place, it had to be tested and Noa found himself holding his breath as the specialist electrophysiologist deliberately put George's heart into the fatal rhythm of ventricular fibrillation in order to check that the device would detect the rhythm fast enough and then deliver the electric shock at the correct level of joules to reset the heart's normal rhythm.

This was the riskiest part of the whole procedure. Noa was staring at the screen of the monitor as the healthy spikes of a normal ECG sped up and changed shape. He felt his own heart skip a beat as the small shock was delivered and the wash of relief made his skin tingle as normality returned.

He pulled off his theatre gear soon afterwards and headed straight back to the ward, where he found Robin wearing an extraordinary Santa hat that coiled above his head like a soft red spring.

'Eva gave it to me, Daddy.'

'Oh?' Noa's glance flicked towards the door. 'Is Eva here?'

'She just came in to give me the hat.' Robin was beaming with pride. 'It's the best hat, isn't it?'

'It sure is.'

Nicole came in as Robin was demonstrating how he could make the pompom bounce.

'I love that hat,' she said. 'Eva wore it on Christmas Day last year when she was on duty. She helped Father Christmas give out all the presents.'

'Will she be helping Father Christmas again this year?' Noa tried to make the question sound casual.

Nicole nodded. 'She's an angel. She's available to fill any gaps that are popping up with people getting sick all over the place. That's why I gave her today off. She's going to spend some time with her family in case she's caught up here in the next few days. But even if she's not needed for a shift on Christmas Day, she usually comes in to join in the fun when Father Christmas is giving out all the gifts.'

Any plan that Noa might have had to ask Nicole for Eva's address went up in smoke. He couldn't even call her now when it might be interrupting time she was having with her own family. And he couldn't desert his own family to go and find her when his parents would be here so soon. And what if Robin was able to go home? That would automatically go to the very top of his list of priorities.

Nicole was certainly grinning at him as if she had something much better to tell him about.

'Blood results are in,' she said. 'I think you're going to be very happy.'

He was. He had a lump in his throat that he needed to swallow before he could smile at Robin.

'I'm going to talk to your other doctors,' he said, 'but I think you're going to be able to have your medicine by just swallowing some pills now. No more needles and you won't need your IV any longer—and you know what that means?'

'What?'

'You'll be able to come home with me.'

'Will I be home before Nana and Grandpa arrive?'

'I think you might be.'

Miriama and Peter Jones weren't the least bit bothered that there were no Christmas decorations up in the house.

'It's you we've come to see,' Noa's father said. 'And our wee Robin. We thought we'd have to come and visit you in the hospital, but here you are—and that's the most amazing Christmas hat you've got.'

'Eva gave it to me.'

'Who's Eva?'

'She's a nurse in my ward,' Noa said. 'And she's been looking after Robin a lot.' But his words felt hollow. Almost a betrayal.

Eva was so, so much more than that.

'She's really nice,' Robin added. He snuggled deeper into the nest of blankets and pillows that Noa had used to make a bed on the couch for him. 'I *love* Eva.'

His grandmother gave him a cuddle. 'I think you love everybody,' she said. 'You're the sweetest boy in the whole wide world.' But she shared a glance with Noa's father that spoke volumes. Were they hoping that Noa might find someone special to share his life with?

That Robin might, one day, have a mother?

'I love Christmas trees, too.' Robin wriggled free of Miriama's embrace. 'There's a really big one at the hospital. Daddy said it might be the biggest tree in the whole wide world.' He looked past his grandmother's shoulder towards the fire with its cheerful flames, but his voice was sad as he added, 'We don't have a Christmas tree.'

'We do,' Noa said. 'And we've got all the decorations for it too. In those boxes. I just haven't had time to unpack them all yet.'

'We can do it tomorrow,' Miriama said reassuringly. 'After we've all had a lovely big sleep.'

'We'll need it,' Noa said. 'Tomorrow's going to be a big day. We've got a bit more grocery shopping to do, too. Did I tell you I've found a place we can get breadfruit and taro? We might not be able to have an umu in the backyard but we can roast them, can't we?'

'Of course we can,' Miriama said happily. 'We've got to have a little bit of Samoa in our Christmas dinner. You were too little to remember, Robin, when you came to New Zealand and we dug the hole in our backyard to cook our Christmas dinner.'

Robin laughed. 'You can't cook a dinner in the ground. It's too cold! It has to go in the oven.'

'You can make an oven in the ground,' his grandfather told him. 'Daddy and I will show you one day, but not this year because the ground *is* too cold to dig holes in on this side of the world. And we need a bit of England in our Christmas dinner too. My favourite is pigs in blankets and they need to go in an inside oven.'

'I want to see Father Christmas.' Robin was tucked up on the couch in front of the fire. 'But I won't be awake when he comes down the chimney, will I?'

'We might wander into the market tomorrow afternoon, then,' Noa said. 'If I give you a piggyback you won't get too tired. I'm sure Nana and Grandpa would love to see all the lights and I think there's a place that you can get your photograph taken with Father Christmas. We could have some hot chocolate, too.'

Oh...the memory of Eva's face as she took that first sip of hot chocolate the day they'd gone to the markets was unforgettable—almost an echo of the way she'd looked just before he'd kissed her that first time—as if she couldn't imagine anything she wanted more. Noa took a quick inward breath as he made his smile morph from poignant to cheerful.

'Would you like to go to the markets, monkey?'

'Yes, *please*, Daddy...'

But Robin was yawning. The excitement of arriving home this afternoon was catching up with him. Noa's parents were yawning, too. They might be asleep before Robin was at this rate. As he reached for his phone to order an early takeaway dinner to be delivered, he thought of something that might keep everybody awake for a little longer.

'How 'bout I wrap you up in your dressing gown and a blanket?' he suggested to Robin. 'We can go outside and find a place to put the bucket of water and some carrots for the reindeer tomorrow night.'

'Ooh…*yes*… Eva told me that she always did that with her daddy when *she* was a little girl.'

His parents shared another glance. 'I hope we get to meet this Eva while we're here,' Miriama said. But Peter gave his head a tiny shake to stop her saying anything else.

'What about a mince pie for Santa?' he asked.

It was Noa's turn to shake his head. He'd totally forgotten to put mince pies on his shopping list. Should he add them to the rather long list of things that needed to be done tomorrow?

No. He'd rather be at the markets with his family, simply enjoying the Christmas spirit. So he smiled. 'Santa's trying to be a bit healthier this year,' he said. 'He'd rather have a carrot.'

Everybody was sound asleep by seven o'clock that evening.

Everybody except Noa.

Very quietly, he was doing what he'd intended doing some time ago. He cut the bindings around the Christmas tree and removed the packaging that was keeping the bottom of it damp. He put it into its hollow metal stand and tightened the bolts to keep it upright, remembering the drama of the hospital tree that had fallen onto the unfortunate Kyle Woodgate and broken his leg so badly. He certainly didn't want anything to fall on top of a small boy who would be so happy to be helping to attach decorations tomorrow.

Noa opened the boxes with those decorations in them and piled them onto the floor beneath the tree in a colourful heap on top of the tissue paper they'd been wrapped in. He'd ordered everything that Eva had pointed out to him—all the pretty wooden ornaments and lots of bells and baubles and fruit. There were miles of fairy lights and long strands of tinsel and, best of all, a lovely shiny star to go right on the top of the tree, but hanging them on the branches could wait until tomorrow. It was the kind of thing best done with the whole family taking part and some Christmas music in the background.

He knew his mother would be busy in the kitchen, baking things that would fill the house with delicious smells of things like cinnamon and ginger and his father would be playing games with Robin that would make them both laugh. It would be a real family time, as Christmas Day would also be, but there would still be something missing.

And...for the first time, Noa knew it was more than how much he would miss Sara.

Robin's mother and his first love would always be a part of their lives and her memory would always be treasured.

But this year he would be missing Eva, who was capable of adding new joy to his life and—just as importantly—to Robin's life as well. His son already loved Eva.

He loved Eva.

It was becoming impossible not to feel that love—and how much he was missing her company—with every new Christmas decoration he was unwrapping. Like the little wooden toy soldiers and the smiling gingerbread people and the stars that sparkled as much as Eva's eyes did when she smiled. For the first time in Robin's life, *this* house was going to be filled with the joy of Christmas and it was all because of Eva's encouragement and her love for celebrating the season of family and friendship.

She'd been right about the fireplace, too. It was perfect for the fir tree garland with its red velvet bows that came out of one of the last boxes, along with some sticky hooks to hang it along the mantelpiece.

The scented candles were in that box as well, and right at the bottom was the stocking, embroidered with Robin's name on the white border at the top. He would help Robin hang that up himself tomorrow, ready to be filled with treats for him to find on Christmas morning.

It was well after midnight when Noa flattened the last of the boxes to put outside for the recycling. It was only then that he found something he hadn't ordered—a complimentary packet of Christmas cards that one of the shops had added to a box of his purchases. Small cards that featured a robin on the front, surrounded by snowflakes enhanced by silver glitter.

Pretty cards.

It was too late to use them this year, however, with less than twenty-four hours before it would be Christmas Day.

Or was it?

Noa opened the packet and took out one of the small cards.

He was going to have a very busy day tomorrow with his family that included finding a way to have a secret dash into town at some point because, also thanks to Eva, he'd finally come up with the perfect Christmas gift for Robin this year. There would be no chance of slipping away to try and find a moment to have a private conversation with Eva, who would probably be far too busy with her patients, anyway.

But…what if he wrote a card and left it at the reception desk at the Royal as they went past on their way to the markets so that someone could deliver it to the paediatric ward?

A card that had a robin on the front of it and an invitation inside to come and visit on a special day, because he—and Robin—would very, very much like to see her?

If she accepted that invitation, it would be the only sign Noa needed that maybe she felt the same way as he was feeling.

She might understand that she was needed.

That she could be loved as much as she deserved to be.

By a man and a little boy.

She might see this message for what it really was—an invitation to become even more of a part of this little family.

CHAPTER THIRTEEN

Christmas Eve

Eva's niece and nephew had decided that the day before the day before Christmas was going to become a family tradition.

Eva's Christmas.

Because that gave them three special days to look forward to. And the bonus of not only an early present but not being expected to eat Brussels sprouts. Hayley loved her Christmas pudding earrings and Eva was wearing hers today, saving her Rudolph the Red-Nosed Reindeer ones for the big day tomorrow. That was when she would also wear her necklace that was a string of tiny red and green lights that flashed so they looked like they were chasing each other around her neck. The tiara of holly leaves and berries might come out then too, as a finishing touch.

Breakfast time was over and done with and Eva was very aware that there was a different little boy in Robin's room. She'd known she was going to miss him because he'd been here for long enough to capture her heart completely, but she also knew there was more to it than the fact that he was an adorable child.

He was Noa's child.

And she loved them both.

She kept her brightest smile on her face as she did the medication round and then accompanied the doctors on duty for the ward round. She helped with some blood tests and soothed a baby who was outraged at having been poked with a needle. It was past time for her to grab a break but it didn't look as if the day shift was going to get any less busy and that was a good thing as far as Eva was concerned. If she wasn't busy, she would have too much time to think.

Too much time to miss having Noa and Robin nearby.

A group of carol singers arrived who wanted to entertain the children. Christmas movies were running back-to-back in the playroom and there was a constant stream of people coming in to leave gifts for the children under the tree Eva had decorated by the reception desk. One of the older paediatricians, Dr Bennett, loved to get dressed up as Father Christmas and he would be here tomorrow to distribute the gifts throughout the ward. Children were, after all, the focus of Christmas everywhere and there were a great many people who wanted to try and help both the children who were stuck in hospital at this time and their families to find as much joy as possible.

It wasn't possible for everyone, of course. There were children who were too sick to have any visitors and families who were too distressed to want anything to do with any celebrations. Eva knew when to take off her headband, slip her earrings into her pocket and, sometimes, to put a gown over her festive scrubs. She did exactly that when a baby was sent up from the emergency department for observation in the paediatric ward due to a potential infection. Baby Alice was only eight weeks old and was accompanied by her frightened parents.

It was Dr Bennett who was on duty today and Eva had the notes from the emergency department ready when he arrived, with Nicole, in the treatment room to do the admission assessment. So far, there was nothing too concerning about the recordings taken. Alice's temperature, blood pressure and heart rate were all normal and her abdomen was soft. She was pale and quiet most of the time but when she did cry, it was with a high-pitched sound that had sounded an alarm.

'We need to get a blood sample to check for signs of infection,' Charles Bennett told the parents. 'We'll insert a very small cannula in her hand or foot or possibly in a vein in her scalp, and that can stay there for any further tests and for giving her any medication she might need.' The senior doctor's tone was sympathetic but firm. 'We also need to do a lumbar puncture to rule out meningitis.'

'No...*please*...she's too tiny...' Alice's mother burst into tears. 'I can't bear it...'

Charles raised an eyebrow at Nicole with an unspoken message that it would be a lot easier for everyone involved if the parents were not present for such an invasive procedure.

'Come with me,' Nicole said. 'Let's leave Alice with Eva, who will take the very best care of her, I promise. She loves babies. This will be over very soon.'

Eva took the infant gently from the mother and cuddled her while the room was set up for what needed to be done. As a bottle-fed infant, Alice was happy to suck on a pacifier, coated with the sucrose that had been proven to help with pain relief for babies.

Charles was a very experienced paediatrician that Eva would have trusted with her own child without hesitation but...

She couldn't help wishing that it was Noa who was doing this procedure. Other doctors could be just as skilled and even more experienced but nobody else could ever have that sense of connection that Noa seemed to have with both his young patients and their families.

He was, quite simply, the best doctor she'd ever worked with.

And the most wonderful man she'd ever met.

She held baby Alice as he found a vein on the top of her foot and gently inserted a very fine needle and cannula. Then she held the baby on the bed, one hand on the small rump and the other on her shoulders, keeping the tiny body in a curve that allowed another small needle to enter the space between two bones in the lower back to extract a few drops of the cerebrospinal fluid.

She remembered every moment of Robin having this test. When he'd been clutching the Santa-elf toy for the first time and snuggling into her arms so that he could have that first needle put in his hand and medications that took care of his pain and anxiety. She could remember being aware of how hard it had been on Noa and knowing exactly how much he adored his son.

Noa had such a big heart. He had so much love to give his family and his patients and still keep space to remember the wife who had been lucky enough to be loved by him for long enough to live the dream of what Noa himself had called the perfect life.

She couldn't blame him for not wanting to ever try and replace that relationship.

But knowing that it could never go any further wasn't going to make a dent in how much she loved him.

It could have been seen as a disaster, Eva thought as she carried baby Alice back to her parents. She'd fallen in love with someone who simply wasn't available and that could have left her with a broken heart for the rest of her life, but she wasn't going to let that happen.

Especially not today. The carol singers were in the ward now and she could hear the harmony of their voices as they sang her favourite Christmas songs like 'Little Drummer Boy' and 'Silent Night' and 'Deck the Halls with Boughs of Holly'.

You could choose to be happy, Eva reminded herself. You could choose to be happy that something wonderful had happened instead of feeling sad that it hadn't lasted as long as you might have wished for.

When she put Alice back into her mother's arms and saw the way the baby's father gathered both mother and child into his arms, Eva could feel the love in that touch.

She settled the little family into the room where Alice would stay under observation until the test results came back and then went back to tidy the treatment room but she was still think-

ing about the way Alice's parents had been holding each other.

She could still feel the way Noa had touched
her the night of Robin's birthday.

In that magical time they'd had together, when
the rest of the world and their normal lives and
all their memories, even, had not intruded in any
way on what they'd discovered with each other.

It hadn't been simply sex. She knew that. No
physical touch could feel that deep unless it
was done with love. Even if Noa wouldn't—or
couldn't—acknowledge that, Eva knew she was
still capable of feeling a love like that. And feeling as if she *could* share her life and love with
someone other than her own family.

She didn't *have* to spend the rest of her life
alone, did she?

She might have convinced herself that she was
happier on her own but that wasn't really true.
She *could* be happy on her own—as she had
been for years now—but how much better would
it be to love and be loved?

The carol singers were standing in front of
the tree beside the reception desk as Eva went
back to check on Alice and...*oh*...the song they
were singing was the haunting melody of 'O
Holy Night' that had brought her to tears when
she'd heard it on the bridge when she was with

Noa and he'd wanted to know what had upset her that day.

Okay...

Maybe she would need to learn to be happy on her own again.

Because there was no one else she could imagine being with, other than Noa Jones.

Or Robin.

She could hold a baby like Alice and cope with the pang of knowing that she would never hold a tiny baby of her own.

But she had held Robin in her arms and known that it was possible to love a child just as much as if she'd given birth to him herself.

Eva wasn't about to start feeling sorry for herself and she didn't have time to for the rest of her shift, anyway. Alice's initial results came back clear but, a couple of hours after her admission, Eva found blood in her nappy. A new examination revealed a mass in her abdomen, an X-ray revealed an obstruction in her bowel and a pelvic ultrasound examination showed the dangerous evidence of an intussusception. A procedure to try and reduce the way a part of the bowel had folded in on itself to cause the obstruction failed and this could only be resolved by emergency surgery to prevent the baby going into shock or suffering from irreversible internal damage.

Eva didn't even suggest the use of the sleigh

bed to take Alice to Theatre. She walked with the parents as they carried their precious baby to deliver her into the hands of the surgeons. And then she waited with them as they held their breath, waiting for news.

And that, too, was a memory of being with Noa.

A memory that Eva was always going to be grateful for because that had been the beginning of the new joy of another person she could love with her whole heart and soul. It might be bittersweet but the joy of being close to someone who made you feel like this was still there, even if you couldn't tell them about it.

There was nothing to stop her caring about Noa.

Feeling privileged to be able to work with him.

Noticing the way the world got a little lighter every time he smiled.

Nothing could ever erase the memories.

And that was a gift Noa had given her, whether he'd intended to or not.

Christmas was in the air all around them.

Miriama Jones was busy in the kitchen from the moment she got up before anyone else and made pancakes for breakfast.

'Oh, my goodness,' was the first thing she said

to Noa when he appeared. 'Did you stay up all night decorating the house?'

'It was quite late by the time I got to bed,' Noa admitted.

'You've even put fairy lights all over the summer house at the bottom of the garden. Must have been a bit cold out there in the middle of the night, but doesn't it look gorgeous?'

It was still dark outside and the kitchen windows looked out on the garden. The little summer house, that was only big enough for a small wicker couch and a low table, was sparkling with lights threaded through the bare branches of the rose that scrambled over its roof and the pretty archway of its entrance.

'It was cold. It even snowed on me at one stage but it didn't settle. Sounds like we might get some more today. Wouldn't that be wonderful? Robin's never seen a white Christmas.'

But Noa wasn't really thinking about the weather at all. He was remembering the first time Eva had been in this house and he'd left her downstairs while he went to fetch Robin's swimming trunks and had another look for Sheepy. He'd had to go looking for Eva when he came back and he'd found her in the conservatory beside the kitchen, admiring the garden.

He wanted her to see the summer house in all its sparkling, fairy, Christmas glory because he knew she would love it. Her whole face would light up with the joy of it and that moment would make the world feel like a happier place.

It would make him feel like a much happier man.

'I haven't either.' His mother's voice broke into his thoughts. 'Funny, isn't it? I've had Christmas in summer my entire life and yet it *feels* more like Christmas when it's in winter. I feel as excited as Robin will be when he wakes up and sees all the decorations and the tree. The garland over the fireplace is perfect and I could smell those candles before I even came into the room.'

Noa turned on the fire to add its warmth and cheer to the dark morning. He lit the candles but Miriama had her first batch of gingerbread in the oven by the time Robin came downstairs so the smell of Christmas spices was almost too much.

Robin certainly looked a little overwhelmed. Wide-eyed, he walked slowly towards the tree and sat on the floor, cross-legged—close enough to touch the mountain of ornaments but he was looking up through the branches of the tree.

'It's nearly as big as Eva's tree,' he said in an awed whisper.

Miriama's eyebrows vanished under the black curls of her hair. 'Eva's tree?'

'He means the one at the hospital,' Noa said. 'Remind me later to tell you the story of the poor guy who pulled the whole tree down on top of him when he was trying to put the star on the top.'

'Can I put the star on our tree, Daddy? *Please?*'

'As long as you don't try doing it by yourself, monkey. I'll be holding onto you, okay?'

It took half the morning to decorate the tree, with Robin supervising the positioning of every decoration and strand of tinsel. Finally, his father held him up in his arms, high enough to hook the star onto the very tip of the tree, and then they all stood back and watched as he flicked the switch and the lights started twinkling.

'*Ohh…*' Robin's eyes were shining just as brightly as those fairy lights. 'It's like magic, isn't it, Daddy?'

It was.

It was perfect.

Almost.

Noa's gaze slid sideways, to the end of the mantelpiece where the stocking was folded up to be hung from the front of the mantelpiece tonight. Beside the stocking was a small red envelope that had Eva's name written on the front of it.

'Let's get tidied up and then into all our warm clothes,' he said. 'I think it's time to go for a walk and see all the special Christmas things out there.' He smiled at Robin. 'Shall we pop into the hospital so that Nana and Grandpa can see the biggest tree in the world?'

'Can we go and see Eva, too?'

'I think she'll be very busy,' Noa said. 'Looking after all the children who are sick.'

'Like I was?'

'Like you were. And you're still getting better so I think you'll need a big nap this afternoon.'

Miriama laughed. 'I think I might, too.' She stooped to pick up some of the tissue paper from the decorations and noticed the pile of cards on the coffee table.

'Oh,' she said. 'Look at these, Robin…they're Christmas cards with you on the front. Lots of little robins. Do you think we might see a real one while we're out today?'

Robin grinned. '*I'm* real,' he told her.

It could have been a sad reminder that the person who'd chosen Robin's name was not with them but they were all laughing and Noa felt his sadness being wrapped in something else.

Gratitude? That Sara had chosen a name for their son that would always make him feel even more special at this time of the year.

Yes. But there was even more gratitude there that he had Robin in his life at all. His son's birth had been a bit of a medical miracle and he'd just had another brush with what could have been a dangerous enough illness for Noa to have lost him.

And Eva had been an important part of that fight for life for this little boy.

She was part of their life now.

Noa wished she was here right now—as part of their family—and the knot of missing her got bigger inside his chest. It made it quite hard to pull in enough of a breath to try and distract them all.

'Do you know why robins are on so many Christmas cards?' he asked.

'Because Robins are special.' Peter scooped his grandson up into his arms for a hug. 'But I think I also heard somewhere that it had something to do with postmen.'

'That's what I heard, too,' Noa said. 'Back in Victorian times, the postmen wore red coats and waistcoats and people called them robins. And they delivered the Christmas cards so they started using the birds as another Christmas theme.'

He stepped closer to the fireplace and blew out the candles for while they were out of the house. Unseen, he slipped the little red envelope into his pocket.

Being a postman himself might be the most important task on the long list of things that needed to be done today.

* * *

Baby Alice's surgery had gone smoothly and after an hour or so in Recovery she was allowed back onto the ward. By that afternoon she was having sips of clear fluids from her bottle and sleeping comfortably in her mother's arms.

'We'll see how she goes after the clear fluid,' Eva told the parents, 'and she might be able to have a little bit of milk later on today. It'll be a few days until you can take her home. I'm sorry—hospital is the last place you want to spend your Christmas, isn't it?'

But Alice's mother was smiling. 'There's way more going on here than there would be at home, to be honest, with real carol singing and everybody getting into the spirit of it all—like you are with those amazing scrubs.'

'I do love Christmas,' Eva admitted. 'Always have, always will. Some of us are just kids at heart.'

'So many people give up their time to try and make it special. It's so lovely to see so many children looking happy even though they're sick. They can't wait for Father Christmas to visit tomorrow. I think we're going to have some special photos to show Alice when she's a bit older.'

Alice's father had tears in his eyes. 'And it doesn't matter where we are as long as our wee girl is going to be okay. It got pretty scary there for a while.'

'I know.' Eva's tone was empathetic. 'But she sailed through that surgery. She's going to be absolutely fine.'

'Is it likely to happen again?'

'It's something that does tend to run in families. And there's a chance it could happen again, but that's something to talk to the surgeon about tomorrow. I'll make sure we remember to bring it up when she does her ward round in the morning.'

'You'll be here?'

'Yes. I'm working tomorrow.'

'Oh, no… I hope you can get some time with your own family.'

'I'm sure I will. I'm about to finish my shift. And have you had a look out of the window this afternoon? It's snowing. Maybe it'll even settle.'

Eva went to the locker room and got well wrapped up with her warm coat and scarf. She reached onto the shelf to pick up her red hat with the stars and touched a tissue-wrapped parcel that was beside it.

Robin's robin. The ornament she'd forgotten to give him yesterday when she'd rushed off after he'd asked her to be his mummy for Christmas.

She knew that Noa's parents would be at his house and she wasn't about to intrude on his family Christmas celebrations, but it was only a short walk away and it would be so pretty to go through the Museum Gardens with flakes of snow drifting down around her before it got too dark. She could just leave the small gift somewhere that Robin would be able to find it, without disturbing anyone in the house. On the doorstep, perhaps?

Nobody needed to know it had come from her. It could simply be another wisp of Christmas magic.

'Eva?' Nicole called as she walked past the reception desk in the ward. 'Something got sent up from Reception for you—hours ago. Sorry, it got buried under some other stuff.' She was holding out a small red envelope. 'I think you have a Christmas card from one of your patients.'

'Oh, that's lovely. Thank you.' Eva took the envelope but slipped it into her pocket.

She was too busy thinking about how she was going to keep this secret mission exactly that.

A secret.

CHAPTER FOURTEEN

THE SNOW WAS falling more heavily now, small flakes that seemed to float and whirl in the air before touching down lightly on a leaf or flagstone.

Noa was watching them as he stood at the kitchen sink washing dishes. His mother had been busy ever since they'd come back from their walk around the central city to admire the lights and let Robin have his picture taken with Father Christmas. She'd prepared the breadfruit and taro to be roasted alongside the more traditional English vegetables like parsnips and potatoes and carrots, wrapped bacon around sausages to be baked for the pigs in blankets and made stuffing for the turkey. A pavlova was in the oven right now, slowly developing the crispy crust over its marshmallow centre, and the kitchen table had wire racks displaying an army of gingerbread people that Robin and his nana had spent the last hour or more decorating with icing and brightly coloured sweets for buttons.

Miriama had given Noa a wink as he'd slipped out of the house for a quick visit to a shop he didn't want Robin to know about. She would keep him happy until he was tired enough to want to curl up for a sleep before dinner, which was what he was doing when Noa arrived home again.

'Did you get everything you needed?'

'I did. I've left it in the back of the car. I'll put it under the tree after he's gone to bed tonight.'

'I might head upstairs myself for a while. It's tired me out, keeping secrets.'

'That's a good idea. I suspect what's really tired you out is a cooking marathon at the same time as keeping your grandson entertained. Thank you so much.' He wrapped his arms around his mother for a quick hug. 'I'm so happy you're here.'

Miriama stepped back far enough to reach up and hold Noa's face between her hands.

'You *look* happy,' she said softly. 'Happier than I've seen you for a long time.'

A quick peek into the lounge after Miriama went upstairs showed Noa that his father had already nodded off where he was sitting on the couch in front of the fire, pretending to read a newspaper. He was glad of a quiet moment to himself and more than happy to spend it washing and drying the mountain of pots and pans, mixing bowls and cooking utensils that had piled up on the kitchen bench.

He looked out of the window again, past the flurries of snowflakes to where his car was parked behind the summer house, and he could feel his lips curving into a smile that was big enough to qualify as a grin. Not only was the weather turning on some potential Christmas magic, what was hidden in the back of his car was going to be the best surprise his son had ever had and that would make it the best one that Noa had ever had as well.

Because when you loved someone as much as he loved his son, what made them happy couldn't fail to make *you* happy as well.

It was one of the best win-win situations that life could bestow.

That smile faded, however, and his eyes narrowed as he caught a flash of colour at the end of the garden that didn't quite fit with the silvery glow of the fairy lights flashing on the summer house.

None of those lights were red.

As red as a robin's breast? Maybe that was what it was. Robins often visited this garden, especially at this time of year when they left food out for the birds.

But then he saw the movement. It was hard to make out the shape behind the combination of the sparkling lights and snowflakes but he felt a chill run down his spine.

Someone was there—in the garden. In the summer house.

Someone who didn't want anyone to know that they were there because they'd snuck in through the gates that led to the road on that side of the property to avoid coming through the house. But why on earth would anyone want to be out there in this weather? And what on earth were they *doing*?

Noa closed the conservatory door quietly behind him as he swiftly left the house, not wanting either Robin or his parents to be alerted to the fact that there was an intruder on their property. And by the time he was more than halfway down the long garden and he could see past the brightness of the fairy lights, he was very glad he didn't have anyone else with him.

Because he could see who it was now.

Eva…

Her name had never sounded quite like that. Like a sigh.

Or perhaps a plea?

Had Noa even intended to say it aloud?

Hearing it had given her a real fright because she had been so focused on her task she hadn't seen the shape of him past the dazzling brightness of the fairy lights right beside her face. The strings she'd been trying to tie onto the strand of lights at the central point of the archway slipped through her frozen fingers as she jumped at the sound of her name and the robin ornament fell into the snow on the path that led to the summer house.

'I'm sorry,' she gasped. 'I shouldn't be here. I—'

'No… *I'm* sorry,' Noa interrupted her. 'I'm so sorry, Eva. And I'm so glad that you *are* here. Did you get my card?'

'Card?' For a moment Eva was bewildered and then she remembered the little red envelope in her pocket. 'Oh, no… I haven't read it…' She fumbled with the pocket on her coat but her fingers were so cold they didn't seem to be working properly. There were snowflakes sticking to them. They were landing on her face too, as she stared up at Noa. Was he really glad that she was here?

It certainly looked as though he was.

'You don't need to read it,' he told her. 'I can tell you what it says. But come out of the snow at least or we'll both freeze.'

Noa stepped through the archway and drew her into the shelter of the summer house, behind the screen of twinkling lights. There were blankets folded up on the ends of the wicker couch and he opened one to pull around them both. He left his arms around Eva, holding the blanket in place. Close enough for the warmth of his body to be doing more to warm her up than the woollen blanket. She could feel his heartbeat.

'It said "Robin and I are both missing you",' he said. 'And "If there's any way you could find time to visit us on Christmas Day, it would make it even more special." I might have added a few kisses at the bottom.'

He looked as if he wanted to smile but couldn't quite manage it.

Had he written that card because Robin had told him about wanting her to be his mummy for Christmas? Was he doing this for his beloved son?

'I'm *so* sorry,' Noa said quietly. 'It was unforgivable the way I walked away from you the other night without even saying anything about…about…'

What did he want to call it?

Getting carried away?

Having sex?

Making love…?

'It's okay,' she whispered. 'I knew there were other things going on. Big things.'

Like Robin.

Like Sara's ghost.

'Too big,' Noa agreed. 'I couldn't get my head

around it so it was easier to take the first escape route I could see and go back to Robin.'

He'd needed to escape from her? He'd used that word before, hadn't he? When he'd made it sound as if leaving her marriage had been a necessary but also brave thing to do.

Eva could feel her eyes fill with tears.

'I couldn't even start to think about how you'd made me feel,' Noa said then, his voice low. 'I never thought I could feel like that again about anyone and…and I felt like I was betraying Sara's memory.'

Eva only nodded once but it made a tear spill and it trickled down her face.

'It was bad enough being so attracted to you,' Noa added softly. 'But I was handling that. It was when I knew that I was falling in love with you that it got too much. I'm sorry…'

Another slow tear followed the first one.

'It's okay,' she whispered again. 'I've done the same thing. I always walk away if I think I'm getting too close. That way, nobody has to find out what a failure I am.'

It was true. It was the best protection she could give herself so that she never felt unwanted ever again.

Unloved.

Not good enough.

'You've never failed,' Noa told her gently.

'You've *been* failed. By your ex. And by me. I realised how wrong I was but I couldn't find the time or a private place to try and tell you that. I couldn't find *you*. Work got crazy and then my parents arrived and then it's been all about trying to celebrate a Christmas that Robin will remember for ever and—'

But Eva wasn't hearing the list. She was stuck on one word.

'*Wrong?*' she echoed. 'What were you wrong about?'

'That I was doing the right thing in not letting anything become as important as being a father. My mother told me. You said it yourself but I wasn't listening properly.'

'What did I say?' Eva was feeling so much warmer now, despite the snow still falling outside the summer house.

'That I had to look after myself. And do things that will help me so that I can be the best dad for Robin. We were talking about me doing my job, but that's not the only thing I need to help me. I thought I could do this on my own. I *wanted* to be able to do it on my own. I had this crazy idea that it would somehow make my love for Sara more real if I never let anyone that close again but…you know what?'

'What?' Without noticing it happening, Eva had wriggled closer as Noa was talking, wanting to feel the rumble of his voice as well as hear it. She was touching his body with her own now. Melting against him.

'I wasn't just hurting myself by doing that. I was hurting the person I love most in the world. I've been depriving Robin of the love he could get from having a whole family around him. I'm preventing him from learning about the kind of relationships that can make adults be the best people they can be. About the support and encouragement and the fun people can give each other and...you know something else?'

Eva knew she didn't need to say anything. Noa was going to tell her anyway.

'That's what Sara would have wanted for both of us. For us to be happy. And...you make us happy, Eva. Both of us...'

The kiss had been waiting to happen. Dancing amongst those snowflakes and just waiting for a chance to settle, and this was it. Eva lifted her chin and Noa dipped his head and brushed her lips with his before letting them settle and move over hers, his breath escaping in a deep sigh of what sounded, and felt, like pure relief.

He'd told her he knew he was falling in love with her.

Eva kissed him back, hoping that he would somehow be able to tell that she *was* already in love with *him*. That this kiss was opening a door to…

Hope, that was what it was.

Hope that this was really happening. That this was the beginning of a brand-new family.

Her very own family. Herself and Noa and Robin.

That she could be his mummy for Christmas. And that she wouldn't be pretending.

Finally, she broke the kiss. Just in case words were needed as well.

'You make me happy, too,' she said. 'And I get it. I had convinced myself that I would be much happier if I was alone. I'd given up hoping for the fairy tale of finding someone to share my life with but… I was wrong, too. It's not the same. Nothing's the same.'

'No.' Noa's arms tightened around her. 'It's not.'

'I mean, I would have gone to the Christmas markets by myself but I would never have ridden on the carousel alone. Having someone to do it with makes it happen. And it makes it… I don't know…bigger? Better? You get to remember it together afterwards and that makes you smile all over again.'

Noa was smiling now. 'I would never have done that without you. I would never have done what I did today if it wasn't for you either.'

Eva's inward breath was a gasp. 'What did you do?'

'I got my mum to distract Robin by decorating gingerbread men and I made a secret dash into the city to buy…dog stuff. A basket and bowls and a harness and lead and…so many things.'

'You're getting a dog?' Eva's eyes widened. 'For Christmas?'

'No. There's a toy dog that'll be under the tree for Christmas. The real one won't be ready to come home for a couple of weeks. It's one of Molly's puppies—the one Robin loved the most at his birthday party. You were right. This garden is more than big enough for a dog. It's big enough for a whole family.'

He stopped talking long enough to kiss her again. Slowly.

So tenderly, a bit of her heart broke—in a good way.

'There's more than enough room for you too, Eva…if you think you'd like that?'

'Oh…' They were happy tears filling her eyes now. 'I don't think there's anything in the world I'd like more. This is the absolutely best Christmas gift I've ever, ever been given.'

'Come inside,' Noa invited. 'I want you to meet my parents. They're going to be so happy to meet you. Robin's been dropping your name into every conversation.'

'Oh…that reminds me. I need to find his gift. I dropped it.' Eva slid out of Noa's arms and away from the shelter of the blanket. She crouched by the archway and brushed snow away to reveal the small bird. 'I bought it in the market that day,' she told Noa. 'I was going to tie it up here and hope that he would see it and think it might be real.'

'Let me.' Noa took the strings of the ornament. His extra height made it easy for him to tie it to hang beneath the string of fairy lights.

They began to walk towards the house, but then Eva turned back. She wanted to see if the little ornament would be easily seen.

What was left of the winter's afternoon daylight was almost gone but, yes, the little robin ornament was glowing in the lights. And…

'Oh, my…' Eva breathed. '*Look…*'

Noa stopped and turned, putting his arm around Eva's shoulders. It wasn't just the ornamental bird they could see. A *real* robin was perched on one of the bare rose branches that framed the archway. Its head was tilted and the bright black eyes were inspecting the imposter. Then it turned and looked at Noa and Eva for a moment before flying away into the deepening dusk.

'They're supposed to bring good luck, you

know,' Noa said softly, pulling Eva close to his side. 'And happiness.'

'I think it's true,' she whispered back. 'I don't think I've ever felt this happy. Or lucky.'

She could hear the smile in Noa's voice.

'Same…'

EPILOGUE

Christmas Eve two years later...

ROBIN WAS A big boy now.

Six years old.

He was going to proper school and he didn't have to take any more pills or go into those scary machines so that they could take pictures of his brain. Daddy said that sore bit in his head that had made him sick was completely better now.

He didn't need to go and see the physiotherapists again and he wouldn't ever have to wear that special helmet in case he bumped his head. He had a woolly hat on today, but on top of that he was wearing the springy Santa hat that was his favourite. The one with the pompom on the top that bounced even if you didn't squash the coil. It was bouncing now, as the pony he was riding went up and down.

He was big enough to be allowed to ride one

of the carousel ponies all by himself this year—
as long as he promised he wouldn't let go of the
twisty pole.

Promises were very important things.

There'd been a lot of promises being made in
the garden this morning in front of quite a lot of
people. When Mummy and Daddy had got all
dressed up and were standing inside the door of
the summer house.

Nana had helped Robin get dressed up as well.

'Because you're a part of this,' she told him.
'This is about your daddy and Eva telling the
whole world that you're going to be a family.
For ever. And you've got a very important job
to do, haven't you?'

Robin's nod had been solemn, but when it
came time for him to do his important job he'd
stopped listening carefully enough and Nana had
to help him find the rings in his pocket.

The promises had gone on a bit too long. That
was why he'd been watching the robin who was
perched on the top of the summer house.

*I promise I will love you with every breath I
take...*

*I promise I will always be by your side, even
if you can't see me...*

*I promise you forever but even that won't be
long enough...*

* * *

He wasn't really riding the pony all by himself.

Daddy was on the pony right beside him. And Mummy was on the pony on the other side of him.

Nana and Grandpa weren't riding the ponies. They said someone needed to look after Holly the dog because she wasn't allowed on the carousel. He could see his grandparents every time the carousel went past the place they were standing, with Holly sitting between them.

They'd called her Holly because she was a Christmas puppy, even though she didn't come home on that Christmas Day. Robin hadn't been born on Christmas Day either and he still had a Christmas name.

Maybe it was just something that his family liked.

They'd told him a secret as they were coming to the market this afternoon and it wasn't that they thought this was the best way ever to celebrate them getting married after everybody else had gone home.

No, the secret was that he was going to get a baby sister.

She wasn't going to be born for a while yet so her birthday wouldn't be anywhere near Christmas, but they were still going to give her a Christmas name.

Ivy.

Robin sat up a bit straighter on his pony. Mummy and Daddy were looking at each other and laughing but he was looking straight ahead.

As if he could see into the future.

He was going to be the *best* big brother in the whole world.

He might even let Ivy wear his springy Santa hat one day…

* * * * *

*Look out for the next story in
the Royal York Hospital miniseries*
Winter Nights with the Midwife
by Karin Baine

*And if you enjoyed this story, check out
these other great reads from Alison Roberts*

Their Fake Date Rescue
Midwife's Three-Date Rule
Paramedic's Reunion in Paradise

All available now!